Melanie Brown was inspired to complete *The Broken Balalaika* after finding several chapters, written in the 1980s, by her late mother, Margaret.

Melanie spent eighteen years of her life, as a photographer, working on a variety of cruise ships sailing all over the globe, and absolutely loved it.

She has now settled in Spain with her son and two Chinchilla cats and spends her time painting animal and nature studies and baking a multitude of cakes.

She is already gathering more memories from her life at sea, and after, for a follow-up book.

To my dearest mother, Margaret, who began this book in the first place.

…and to the real Gennadi.

Margaret and Melanie Brown

THE BROKEN BALALAIKA

Based on a True Story During
the Cold War

AUSTIN MACAULEY PUBLISHERS®

LONDON · CAMBRIDGE · NEW YORK · SHARJAH

A CIP catalogue record for this title is available from the British Library.

ISBN 9781035886388 (Paperback)
ISBN 9781035886395 (ePub e-book)

www.austinmacauley.com

First Published 2025
Austin Macauley Publishers Ltd®
1 Canada Square
Canary Wharf
London
E14 5AA

To all my friends who encouraged me on this revisited journey.

Table of Contents

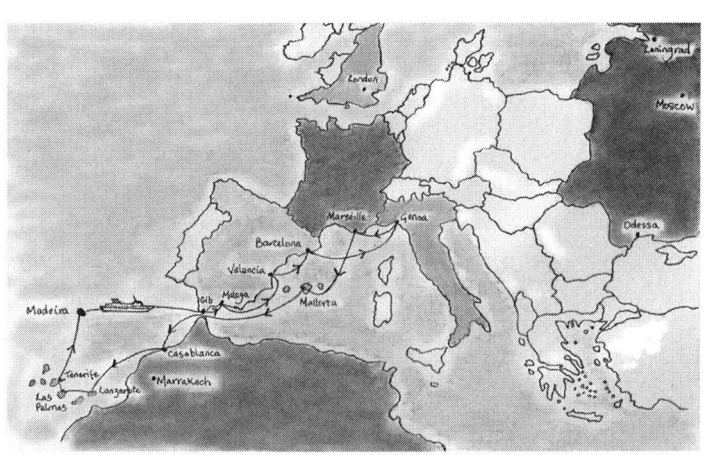

The Route of the *Ukraina*

Prologue

In the catalogue of human events, recklessness must be responsible for many decisions, which, under different circumstances, might never have been taken. Just such an emotion occupied my mind, as I sat at the bar of the MS *Ukraina* sipping Cointreau, cruising somewhere between Casablanca and Lanzarote. As a result, I was just about to make a decision which would radically change my life and that of another person on the liner, who at that time was quite unknown to me. I was completely unaware any such momentous event was about to be instigated, especially when the instigator was my close friend and colleague, Dermot.

My name is Louisa Bennett. It was 1981. I was 21 years old and one of the first single women to enter a definitive man's world on a Russian passenger liner—a Soviet ship.

1

City of Spices

It had been a long and tiring day. Everyone was up at 7am for the excursion to inland Morocco; a lengthy coach journey from Casablanca, of several hours, in the comparative cool of the early morning and arriving in Marrakech to the blinding heat of the *Djemaa e Fna* on a day in late August.

Although I regularly visited this noisy, colourful square crammed with Arab traders and multinational tourists, overflowing into the winding *souks* leading from the city centre, I never failed to sense the great excitement of the place. The loud guttural calls of the traders, as locals and foreigners pushed their way through the narrow lanes of closely packed stalls, selling beautifully polished copperware and shining silver tea sets, intricately woven jewel-coloured carpets and glittering Moroccan *djellabas*. Then turning a corner and entering the food quarter, we would be greeted with multiple rows of perfectly stacked ripe oranges and bowls of freshly picked mint leaves, surrounded by mountains of exotic spices, spectacularly vibrant, assailing the senses and mingling their fragrances with those of illicit aromas from a hundred Arab pipes.

But I was not in Marrakech to soak up the atmosphere and enjoy the scenery. I was a ship's photographer, whose duty it was to accompany the passengers on shore excursions and take as many interesting and artistic shots as time would allow. The *souks* were ideal for atmospheric compositions and the passengers particularly liked the candid shots I took, as they haggled with the local traders for various souvenirs to take back to the ship. Sometimes the group would stop for a refreshing cup of mint tea as they sat on soft leather pouffes, whilst Moroccan men tried their hardest to sell some 'Aladdin' type carpets.

Soon it would be time for lunch amidst a balmy hibiscus-laden garden on the veranda of an elegant hotel, where we would be treated to a feast of North African specialities—a selection of pureed dips and unleavened bread, lamb couscous with dried fruit and nuts or a mildly spiced chicken *tagine*. This was always followed by sweet honey pastries and more mint tea, served from an elegant silver teapot, skilfully poured by the waiter from a ridiculously high height, splashing with amazing accuracy into each of our small glasses below.

Then on retiring to an indoor area, with soft divans positioned along the walls, covered in silken decorative cushions, we made ourselves comfortable for a very special performance. I prepared my camera as a group of local musicians padded in and seated themselves on the sumptuous rugs at one end of the room, complete with small drums and a variety of Moroccan stringed instruments. As they began to play, we heard the sound of many tiny bells jingling, just outside the door and as the noise grew louder, all eyes turned to feast on the figure that whirled and spun her way into the room. Dressed in coloured silks, with shiny gold discs attached to her bodice, ankles and waist, she dazzled and shone like a beautiful tropical bird. Shaking her ample breasts and tossing her silky, dark, hair she twirled and shook her generous hips, midriff bare, metallic discs jangling and catching the light—totally bewitching and mesmerising her enthralled audience.

A roar of approval greeted her finale as she collapsed on the floor in an elegant pose. And more applause followed as she proceeded to invite a few brave guests to join her and endeavour to emulate her spectacular, gyrating hips and flamboyant movements. Dissolving into fits of laughter, the novice dancers soon returned to their seats, whilst the belly dancer made a final shimmering spin and disappeared swiftly in a flurry of glittering silks.

Thoroughly satisfied with the day's excursion, a happy but weary group gathered again by the buses for the return trip back to the ship. As the last passenger climbed aboard the coach, a flushed and panting figure bounded up—it was Dermot.

'Can I cadge a lift on your bus, Lou?' he asked with an apologetic look. 'I saw mine disappearing in a cloud of dust as I ran back from the *casbah*!' he added with a slight grin.

It turned out that Dermot had been delayed as a result of an even longer than usual haggling session with the wizened little Moroccan who supplied him with the comfy, soft moccasins that had been his adopted style of footwear for all the time I had known him. I couldn't ever recall seeing his feet in anything else. He sank into a spare seat next to me, whilst the guide counted heads yet again and signalled to the driver that we could leave. The bus then started to slowly negotiate its way through the ever busy and bustling streets.

Marrakech, in the early evening, is teeming with life and it took all the skill, experience and patience of the driver to avoid pedestrians, dogs, donkeys, cyclists and even the odd stately camel, as we headed for the coast, homeward bound. The town eventually behind us, the coach was able to speed up on the long straight road to Casablanca and the more settled motion lulled most of the occupants into fitful sleep.

Dermot gazed at the roof of the bus, closed his eyes and sighed deeply. 'Lou, darling. Why am I such a damned good photographer?'

I smiled. I'd heard this opening remark many times before. 'Dermot, you are actually a very good photographer but you're not much of a darkroom technician. Do you want me to put the films through tonight and you can print them off in the morning while I sell in the shop?'

'Brilliant idea, Lou. I'll just have a quiet night and hit the sack early.'

A couple of years working with Dermot had established his character fairly well. He was indeed a good photographer, but he was never happier than when he was at the bar with his *teploye pivo* (warm beer), his moccasins resting on the stool, as he chatted in a mixture of Russian and English to the bartender.

His eyes were closed now behind his tortoiseshell-rimmed glasses and as I studied his relaxed expression, I remembered when, early on in our friendship, we had considered an affair. We were both healthy, attractive young people with no ties, but something had held us back and I was glad it had because as a result, there was now a man in my life who was a trusted friend, with no deeper emotional involvement to complicate our relationship.

Indeed, our friendship had already been tested when Dermot fell for a beautiful Russian girl working onboard and was now determined to marry her, despite a definite coolness towards the idea from both the Russian authorities and our boss back in England. But I had encouraged them to persevere with their plans—I knew Katya well enough to believe her affection for Dermot was genuine and lasting. His wandering eye had never rested on a girl for so long—a sure sign. It had all taken much longer than either of them had anticipated but at last the formalities seemed complete. After about a year of endless form-filling, the marriage was set for December, only four months away. I was invited to the wedding in Odessa, of course, not only as an official witness but to take photos of the happy event. I was determined to be there.

I glanced at the now sleeping form beside me, his copper-coloured, shaggy hair, his fair smooth skin and neatly trimmed ginger beard, all so familiar and so very English. I wondered how his life would change, once he had a Russian wife and a home in the Soviet Union or maybe England.

The bus was dimly lit, and the excited chatter had now ceased. Only the constant drone of the engine prevailed and soothed most of us into an uncomfortable but unavoidable sleep.

Sometime later, the bus changed tone and began to slow down. Lights flashed by outside and I opened my eyes to see that we had reached the outskirts of Casablanca and soon the familiar ship's funnel, bearing the yellow hammer and sickle on a red background, would be in view—always a welcome sight and one to which I had become accustomed, since working on the Russian ships these past two years.

Safely back on board and with the lights of Casablanca fading along the shoreline, the dining room had just closed its doors and the last of the passengers had retired from the public lounge. All the films we had taken that day had been processed and were hanging in the darkroom, waiting to be printed the following morning.

I thought I might have Dermot for company as I sipped my nightcap in the late-night Kalinka Bar, but he must have returned to his cabin after dinner or disappeared below decks to see his Russian friends. He seemed to be accepted there and tolerated by the ship's staff captain, but none of the other Western staff dared follow his example. We all knew the rules—East and West must not mix socially, and certainly not in private. Our jobs, and the Russian crew's privilege to travel abroad, would be forfeit.

I was, nevertheless, rather envious of Dermot's freedom and was seriously contemplating these restrictions, as I drained the last drop of Cointreau and was just about to bid Sergei, the bartender, *spakoini nochi,* when an arm slipped around my waist and a light kiss brushed my cheek.

'Darling, the night is still young!' said Dermot softly, as he proceeded to order his beer and another drink for me, looking excited and obviously bursting with news that I was just about to hear. 'On my way down to the cabin, Lou, I heard *balalaikas* playing, deep baritone voices singing and the clinking of glasses—in other words, a crew party. Care to go?' he added nonchalantly.

I threw back my head and laughed. 'Oh, Dermot, you're quite impossible! I'd like nothing better than to go but you know as well as I do, it's more than my job's worth to get involved with the crew.' I felt my heart starting to beat a little too fast as I considered this enticing invitation, and swallowed the last of my Cointreau in one gulp, making me cough slightly.

Dermot finished his drink saying, 'Come on, darling, just this once, no one need know. There's hardly anyone around and you can't possibly go to bed this early. After all, their door is right next to yours. They're bound to keep you awake!'

He was right. I had often heard snatches of music from behind the metal door at the end of the passageway, when I returned to my cabin late at night, but I had never seen what lay beyond. Normally, I would never have considered disobeying the rules I had always accepted from my employer. I loved my work too much to risk losing it all; but tonight, things seemed different, and I was ready for excitement, which was only needing a little encouragement.

Dermot insisted again, 'Oh, come on, Lou. You'd enjoy yourself—for an hour or so.'

If I'd had the slightest inkling of the events which were to develop from that moment, I would probably never have left the bar with Dermot and headed down to the forbidden crew quarters. My life was about to enter a new and exciting chapter but also a very dangerous one.

2

Out of Bounds

The brightly lit corridors of the ship were deserted as Dermot and I, firmly holding my hand in his, made our way down the wide, red-carpeted staircases descending to the lower decks. The ship's decor was that of a sumptuous hotel with Russian folk-art overtones; thick pile carpets in glowing, jewel colours, expensive wallpaper simulating marble in reds and greens, discreet down-lighters illuminating great banks of exotic plants, all fresh and well cared for.

The large open reception area, where the passengers entered the ship from the gangway, was one deck below the main public rooms and particularly impressive. A large central pillar surrounded by deep-buttoned, banquette seating, upholstered in glowing gold velvet, dominated the scene and the black intricately worked wrought iron balustrade, sweeping upwards from the far side of the hallway, framed the stair of vibrant burgundy. The walls were hung with thick tapestries, glinting with gold embroidery and seeming to glow with rich icon colours.

Here in these beautiful surroundings were the essential offices of the ship for the passengers' information—the cruise director, the excursion desk, the photoshop and the purser's office. And leading on from these was an elegant arcade of shops, full of tempting gifts, from *matryoshka* dolls, lacquered boxes and embroidered Russian shawls to toiletries, perfumes and chocolates—all guaranteed to stop the passengers in their tracks before they reached their allocated cabins.

Heading down the staircases of two more decks, Dermot and I turned into a corridor and faced a passage of four cabins, two of them in fact our own. At the end of the corridor, there was a fifth door of solid proportions, with a large sign attached, stating *Ekipazh* (crew). This was very familiar to me as I passed it every day, and Dermot, pausing only to glance over his shoulder, pushed the heavy bulkhead door slightly open and sure enough, the unmistakable sounds of a party floated up. Putting his finger to his lips and his arm around my waist, Dermot gently manoeuvred me ahead of him, through the partly opened door and following closely behind, we quietly stepped into another world.

The surroundings I had come to accept in the areas of the ship the passengers knew had abruptly vanished. Everything around us was spotlessly clean but severely functional; grey and white linoleum ran the length of the corridor floor, and the walls and ceiling were painted a uniform pale grey. Strong bulbs illuminated the scene and an open companionway led down to the lower decks. Overall, the persistent hum of the engines was very noticeable and blending with it, the sound of ever-increasing handclapping, encouraging some feat of drinking or dancing or possibly a combination of the two. We descended the steep companionway and Dermot, going ahead, stopped briefly at the entrance to the mess. Then, beckoning me to follow, stepped cautiously over the threshold.

All the crew appeared crowded into the room, many sitting at a circle of tables round an improvised stage. The now deafening rhythmical clapping was accompanying a sailor, obviously the worse for the contents of the vodka bottle he was now balancing on his forehead, whilst executing a Cossack dance in the centre of the floor. Everyone was so engrossed in the spectacle that we were able to blend in with the crowd, unnoticed to begin with.

Dermot had many friends amongst the crew because of his relationship with Katya but I had only a working knowledge of the Russians, with an occasional drink at the bar with an officer of rank in full view of his superiors. Several of the male crew I encountered were quite attractive, from the pale-skinned, fair-haired Slavic featured northerners, to the smouldering dark looks of the men from Georgia and other southern, Soviet lands. But almost all of the crew aboard these ships had wives, husbands and families back home and any deviation from the Soviet regulations, could result in a punishment for the crew member involved, or their family.

I had no desire to become entangled in an affair that could lead to suffering and the curtailing of privileges that the Russians on a cruise ship enjoyed. Dermot's girlfriend had been gently dealt with but nevertheless, she had been sent ashore in Odessa, her passport confiscated and instructed to remain in her hometown, until all the formalities of the marriage preparations had been completed.

Occasionally, an engineer or electrician would appear at the information desk to attend to a technical problem, or a crew member might pop by the darkroom to collect a film, never dallying for longer than was necessary. But for the most part, I had never set eyes on the vast number of crew who actually manned the *Ukraina*.

As I looked around with interest, I thought I *did* recognise some of the faces in the room and suddenly recalled where I had seen them before. Though the ship's entertainment programme included professional cabaret acts, the passengers' favourite performers were the talented crew members, who performed in traditional folkloric costumes at the end of every cruise. These would include male and female singers, *balalaika* players and pretty female folk dancers dressed in bright floral outfits, with high red boots and colourful flower garlands round their heads. The highlight of the show was the finale, when a group of Cossack performers would bound onto the stage and whirl, leap and spin high in the air, mesmerising the rapt audience, as each passenger recognised their own cabin steward or waiter in the electrically charged atmosphere.

As I was gazing at several people around me in gradual recognition, I realised that a similar reaction was taking place in the minds of those nearest to me and a burly figure detached itself and greeted me, '*Dobryi viaycher* Louisa, *kak dela?*' And then in English only slightly accented. 'May I get you a drink?'

I smiled at Sergei, more familiar in his smart red waistcoat and bowtie behind the bar I had so recently left, several decks above. I began to wonder how he had arrived at the party so quickly, then reminded myself that his shift being over, he must have promptly caught the crew lift down to the lower deck and beaten us to it.

A glass was in my hand, and I made my way over to Dermot, already settled on a stool and chatting in fractured

Russian to a pretty, dark-haired beauty whom I recognised as Nina, the pleasant little stewardess who sometimes tidied the cabins on our deck. The young Russians were all too obviously delighted to welcome the two gate-crashers. I caught myself wondering why so many restrictions were forced upon them by those in authority and yet how easy it was to integrate when opportunity arose.

There was a cry of welcome from the doorway and yet more members of the crew, recently off duty, arrived to join them. It was difficult to see clearly but this time I thought the newcomers were quite unknown to me. The light fell upon their faces as they came further into the room, and I was able to study each in turn.

The first two were tall, fair-haired and blue-eyed from a Baltic port originally but as occasionally happened, transferred to service with the Black Sea fleet of liners. They were deftly passing a *balalaika* over the heads of the crowd near the door, when I noticed a third member following them and it wasn't until he had come far enough into the room, that the light could properly illuminate his features. When it did, he was standing almost directly across the little dance floor from me, and I looked up into the darkest brown eyes I had ever seen. He smiled and even white teeth gleamed below a long, dark moustache. His skin was tanned and his hair very dark and thick, tamed to regulation length. He seemed as intent on studying me as I was him and only the arrival of his *balalaika*, in the hands of his companion, followed by an instant roar for a song from all the company, broke our concentration.

I discovered that I had been holding my breath and smiling for longer than I'd intended and Dermot, ever watchful, had not failed to notice this wordless exchange.

Leaning forward, he breathed in my ear, 'Gennadi Potenko, electrician, native of Odessa, probably married.'

Thinking I was past such emotions, I felt myself blushing at my transparency and was grateful to the sailor who, with a flourish, placed a stool in the centre of the floor and with an exaggerated sweep of his hand, indicated to Gennadi that the stage was his.

The lights were dimmed, and he sat in a casual, relaxed manner, lit only by an overhead light and began to sing a gentle love song from his Ukrainian homeland. The burst of applause that greeted the familiar opening notes quickly died away and a rich, baritone voice filled every corner of the room. I shrank back into the shadows and listened, captivated, as was the whole room. He sang with such deep conviction and such sincerity that several eyes were moist with homesickness and I, barely understanding the words, was deeply touched.

At the closing passage of the song, Gennadi looked towards the shadowy corner where I sat motionless and addressed the final words I thought, to me. A few more melancholy notes on the *balalaika* and he slowly lifted his long, sensitive fingers from the strings. A moment's pause, complete silence, followed by a roar of approval and a smiling Gennadi, accepting the ovation with an embarrassed wave, vacated the stage and melted into the enraptured audience.

I was clapping as loudly as everyone else and only rested my hands, when I saw the handsome singer was making his way through the congratulatory crowd around him, directly towards me. He stopped within inches of me, smiled and said in Russian, 'Good evening. Would you like something to drink?'

3

The Beginning

The sun was climbing a sky scrubbed clean and streamed into the cabin through the porthole window, rousing me from a restless sleep, shrouded in misty memories and the last remnants of a dream. As I struggled to open my eyes, still heavy with sleep, I felt incredibly thirsty. Turning on my side and through half closed eyes, I saw a deep pink haze on the bedside table. Making a more determined effort to focus, I realised I was looking at a single full-bloom pink rose standing in a glass tumbler. The sheer incredibility of such a sight in mid-ocean slowly filtered into my mind and as my thoughts became clearer, all the events of the past evening crystallised in my brain.

Sitting up quickly and immediately regretting it, I fell back onto the pillows, and it became evident that I was gripped by a hangover of gigantic proportions and of an intensity I had never before experienced. Very slowly and carefully and feeling distinctly nauseous, I slipped from the bunk and headed in the general direction of the loo, and what I hoped would be a reviving shower. It proved a painful few minutes but at least I could see straight when I emerged, a towel draped loosely around my body as I searched for my watch to check the time. Though the sun-filled cabin told even my half-functioning senses that it was already late, I was surprised to see that my watch was not in its usual place by my bed.

Glancing around the cabin, I noticed that it was amazingly tidy and my clothes from the night before, black velvet trousers, black waistcoat and white silk shirt, had been carefully placed on a chair in the corner. I didn't even remember getting undressed and putting them there, nor did I know how I returned to my cabin after the events of the crew party.

I sat down on my bunk and gazed again at the neatly folded clothes and saw my watch sitting on top of the pile. Had Dermot been responsible for this? Had he helped me back and put me to bed? Surely not, if my clothes were anything to go by—Dermot was not the tidiest of men. So that left only one alternative. I had spent the early hours of the morning with Gennadi Potenko conversing in my basic Russian as I soon discovered he knew no English. It had seemed of little importance, the language barrier, for we had spoken with our eyes, and no one had attempted to interrupt and spoil our liaison.

As at all Russian parties, the vodka had flowed and I had fallen victim to its effects. I vaguely remembered standing up to leave and swaying towards Gennadi, then nothing seemed clear, and I knew it would never be, until I saw him again.

A loud knocking interrupted my thoughts and Dermot's voice called out, 'Louisa, have you surfaced yet? It's after breakfast time.'

'Coming,' I called in a faint voice. Even that one word was quite an effort and feeling decidedly frail, I got up from my bunk and opened the door.

He breezed in, apparently quite unaffected by the amount of alcohol he had consumed the night before, looked at me and said, 'What happened to you then, darling? Couldn't prise you away from that singing electrician. You two certainly hit it off. Did he bring you back here?'

'I have no idea, Dermot.' I sighed and sat down again. 'Nor have I any idea how I got myself into bed. When did you last see me?'

He thought for a moment as he joined me on the bunk. 'About three I suppose. I thought we should slip back up here just in case we got spotted by the wrong person. I asked you if you were coming but you certainly weren't interested— more immediate ideas on your mind if I recall.' He slipped an arm around me and gave me a comforting squeeze.

'Oh, Dermot. You should have made me go with you.'

'Made you? What a joke! Anyway, I don't think Gennadi would have allowed it!'

I smiled weakly whilst Dermot considered the implications. 'Do you mean to say, Lou, that he brought you back up here himself? A bit risky if he'd been seen.'

'Of course, it was risky, Dermot, but I think he must have. My clothes were laid on that chair and,' I paused, a little embarrassed, 'there's this rose by my bed. I know nothing about it.'

Dermot craned his neck to see around me and whistled softly. 'Where the hell did he get that in the middle of the Atlantic? Got to hand it to these Ruskies, you know, damn clever people!'

'Dermot! Don't be funny. It's pretty serious. What if anyone *had* seen him? He must have practically carried me back here and I don't remember a thing!'

Dermot then asked the question in both our minds. 'I wonder how long he stayed?'

I laughed ruefully. 'You know the condition I was in. I should think he was glad to get rid of me. I can assure you. I wouldn't have been worth spending the rest of the night with!'

'Well, darling, I don't know how you're going to find out what indiscretions you actually committed. It's not going to be easy to see him again—if you want to, that is.'

'Of course, I want to. I must thank him for getting me back here for one thing.'

'And for another?' he asked shrewdly.

I shrugged my shoulders. 'I can't think straight yet, I don't know anything about him—it's all been so quick. I've never felt like this before.'

'Now look here, Lou, don't you go getting romantic ideas. You're going to get nowhere with a Russian sailor who's already married. Take off the rose tints, darling, it's morning now.'

I turned quickly away from him. 'I think I'll get dressed now, Dermot, and head up to the photoshop. Thanks for looking in. See you for lunch.'

As I glanced back, his face grew serious and he seemed about to say more but he thought better of it, patted my shoulder and quietly left the cabin.

In the silence, I could hear the throb of the ship's engines and wondered if Gennadi was somewhere on the deck below, following his daily routine. My gaze shifted to the pink rose, its petals trembling slightly with the ship's vibration. I smiled to myself. Maybe he was thinking a little of me too.

Then standing up and turning to the wardrobe, I chose a crisp white outfit to wear to face the day.

4

The Message

People choose to spend their vacation cruising upon the waters of this planet for many reasons. Some to recharge and rejuvenate themselves, to escape completely from landlocked distractions of their routine daily lives—the workplace, telephone or commuting. Some seek the timeless quality of the ocean slipping by, the days echoing the rhythm of the tides, the exhilaration of the sheer space all around them. Others just want to experience the ambience of a great liner; the lifestyle, the entertainment, the food, the fascination of exotic ports of call, which before were just pinpricks on a map. Whatever the reasons, passengers who embark on such a holiday must have each day offered to them, each hour filled for them and allowed to choose how they will spend it.

Today was a sea day and that entailed a whole twenty-four hours of cruising between two ports, as the distance was usually too much to cover overnight. This gave the passengers time to recover sufficiently from the land excursions and to enable the ship to generate revenue at the bars, casino, spa and shops. It was also an opportunity for the Russian crew and European staff to demonstrate their service skills and ensure that each guest was catered for, according to his or her taste.

The ship's activities for the day had already commenced and the atmosphere on board was filled with excited people, making their way to various parts of the ship, where a range of sporting events was organised. The mellow voice of the cruise director filled the corridors as she announced the morning's programme on the ship's tannoy system and wished everyone an enjoyable day at sea.

On the back deck, there was clay-pigeon shooting and deck quoits. The portside had a shuffleboard tournament. Starboard deck offered table-tennis for all levels and on the top deck, an aerobics class was underway.

As I left the dining room, I smiled at the sparsely clad guests, making their way to the sun deck for a morning of relaxation and tanning. Soon the waiters would offer them special cocktails and caviar or *pirozhki* savouries, to satisfy their needs before lunch was served. I checked my watch and saw I had half an hour before opening the shop and Dermot would start bringing up the prints, from the previous day's shooting, to be hastily displayed on the boards for the eager passengers' purchase.

My headache and thirst had been briefly allayed by the masses of lemon tea I had drunk at breakfast, even managing a slice of toast. Much to the surprise of Ivan, my steward, who was used to bringing me tasty, cooked eggs from the galley and an array of cured meats and cheese.

A feeling of weariness overcame me as I contemplated sitting in the busy photoshop for three hours, chatting to passengers and trying to help them with the usual camera problems. So, on impulse, I made my way to the boat deck, where I hoped there would be a refreshing sea breeze, to help dispel the remnants of my self-inflicted disposition.

A kind passenger held open the door to the deck for me and I stepped outside to a cloudless blue sky and a reviving cool draught of sea air. Walking towards the railing, I took deep, salty breaths and felt my head gradually clearing, as the wind lifted my hair and stroked my face and neck with unabashed sensuality.

The swish of the ship cutting easily through the silky blue waters of the Atlantic soothed my senses, as I gazed dreamily at the distant, misty horizon. I was vaguely aware of a low conversation in Russian taking place, somewhere nearby. The murmuring continued and I was enjoying the flowing cadence of the exchange and tranquillity of my surroundings, only to be jolted out of my reverie by the thudding of soft-soled shoes on the wooden deck and a peal of laughter as a group of joggers raced by.

Startled, I turned around abruptly and smiled as the leader gave me a jolly wave and disappeared around the corner, nearly colliding with a waiter and a trayful of drinks. This produced more merriment from the group and a tight-lipped smile from the waiter, who hurried past me muttering words in Russian I had never come across before.

I was about to move towards the door leading to the ship's interior, when I heard a tapping noise and looked in the direction of a lifeboat, directly above. There seemed to be some maintenance being carried out on the pulley system and catching sight of the workmen, I was surprised to have my glance returned very enthusiastically by a good-looking blond seaman. This sailor and his companion were obviously the source of the muted conversation I had heard earlier and puzzled, but not wanting to appear rude, I allowed myself the hint of a smile in their direction, which was instantly echoed a thousand-fold. As if accepting an invitation, which I had certainly not intended to issue, the blond man made his way quickly along the side of the lifeboat, swung down and landed with athletic grace, right beside me.

I stepped back in surprise as he looked around warily, then spoke only three words in English. 'Fishing trip, tomorrow.' Another beaming smile, an almost balletic leap up onto the lifeboat and he was back on the maintenance job, almost before I could draw breath.

Gripping the rail tightly, my initial confusion slowly receding as the probable meaning of this encounter began to dawn on me. My spirits became buoyant, my anxiety disappeared and my heart sang. I was also cured of my hangover.

5

Volcanic Isle

Just off the African coast, the Canary Islands bask in a climate favoured by trade winds which waft to the approaching sea voyager, the perfumes of hundreds of tropical flowers. The most northerly of these islands is Lanzarote. Its small capital of Arrecife boasts a harbour too shallow to cope with anything larger than fishing boats and pleasure craft; sea-going liners must berth at a deep water harbour a little way from the town. Here one could also see a large seafood canning factory, which provides employment for a good section of the local population.

After a day at sea, the first excursion ashore in the Canaries was always extremely popular. The passengers would be gathering excitedly on the main deck, immediately after breakfast, to hurry down the gangway as soon as the ship had been cleared by shore officials. I elected to do gangway shots that morning and was first off the ship to tie my life-ring at the bottom, with 'Lanzarote' printed in bold letters across it. I took my place and gaily encouraged the guests to smile in my direction, endeavouring to catch each one, as they eagerly stepped ashore onto the sun-drenched dockside.

As the last passengers on the tour hurried to board the bus, a long-legged figure appeared at the top of the gangway and waved casually to the tour escort to wait a moment.

'Good morning, darling,' said Dermot, as he smiled and came closer, lowering his voice, 'all ready for a day in Lanzagrotty? See you at the Sheraton for a drink about 1pm.'

He didn't wait for a reply but strode over to the last bus and climbed aboard. Then they were off to share the delights of the Fire Mountain. Few visitors to Lanzarote wanted to miss the opportunity of crossing the stark lunar landscape, on the swaying back of a haughty camel, a volcanic furnace still glowing a few feet beneath their plodding feet. I waved back at Dermot and laughed. A light breeze, so typical of Lanzarote blew seductively from offshore, ruffling my bushy hair and rippling over my body with unexpected pleasure. A new exhilaration and glowing sensation overcame me.

Dermot saw it too and looked upwards and I imagined him groaning and wondering what had transpired yesterday to bring about such a change of mood. He knew, as well as I, of the problems lying ahead for myself and Gennadi Potenko, if we chose to follow a certain path. I chided myself inwardly for making my feelings so patently obvious and watched the tour bus as it pulled away noisily, heading for Arrecife along the potholed road.

As I boarded the ship and made my way to the pool bar for a quick coffee before my darkroom duties, I noticed an unexpected sound from the starboard lifeboat deck. It was causing quite a stir of interest, as the remaining sunbathing passengers had left their sunbeds to gather at the railing. I hurried over to join them, a sharp thrill of anticipation running through me as I suddenly realised the meaning of yesterday's message at last.

I had heard this unusual noise only once before on a calm day in the Mediterranean, when the captain had decided to test the lifeboats by lowering them into the sea. I should have known yesterday when I saw the crew checking the boat. Of course, that was the answer. They were using a lifeboat to take some of the crew on a fishing trip in the bay, whilst they were docked in such an ideal harbour. I watched as more of the lucky crew members came up on deck and scrambled into the lifeboat, laughing and exchanging comments in Russian, some of them waving to the amused passengers gathered above.

I scanned the scene as casually as I could, trying not to give the impression that I was looking for anyone in particular. My gaze then shifted to the lifeboat, now being fended clear of the pristine white side of the ship, by a crew of bronzed sailors. They looked relaxed and happy to escape, temporarily, the restraint of their lives on board and behave like any other fishermen in the harbour. The lifeboat crew nearest the ship, reversed their oars and began to pull strongly in harmony with their colleagues, sailing out into the bay.

In the bow, a figure stacked the fishing tackle and sat athwart a coil of rope, his bare feet balancing on each bulwark. He shouted a laughing rebuff at the sailor in front of him who, not used to handling an oar, sent a plume of water up into the sky to catch the sun and descend like silver rain onto his companion. He shook himself dry and wiped the sea water from his face, throwing back his head, and as he did so, my heart leapt.

Gennadi was smiling up at us and the passengers were laughing, and I couldn't help joining in and smiling back, as his eyes reached mine in enraptured surprise. All of a sudden, there were no passengers, no other fishermen, just a handsome man in a small boat, the sun beating down, the sea sparkling and a desire that was escalating beyond my control.

6

The Rescue

I knew that whatever plans Gennadi had, there was no chance of us meeting ashore alone. The crew were only allowed to go out in groups—hardly conducive to a romantic encounter. Ideas chased through my mind, as the lifeboat pulled further away and headed along the coastline towards the headland, surmounted by the hotel where I was to meet Dermot later that day.

The episode over, the passengers drifted back to their sunbeds, happily looking forward to some delicious fresh fish for dinner. I picked up a coffee from Sasha at the pool bar and made for the darkroom, for half an hour of film processing in readiness for printing later on.

The negatives hanging up to dry, I hurried to the cabin to change into my new gold bikini, topping it with blue Bermudan shorts and a t-shirt bearing the ship's name in red. Grabbing a shoulder bag and a magazine, I sprinted up the stairway and almost danced down the gangway ashore. I planned to walk to Las Salinas Hotel about three quarters of a mile away, perhaps have a swim on the way and dry off in the sun, before meeting Dermot.

The rough road was bordered by low scrubby hills, spiked with the occasional brilliantly coloured flower, the almost constant wind blowing a soft layer of dusty soil across it. On the sea side, a slope of sand swept down to the blue ocean and upon it lay sun worshippers, some in bright swimwear, others topless with skimpy, bikini pants. Shading my eyes with my hand, I could see the fishing party quite clearly now out in the bay and even hear odd snatches of laughter, carried landward on the breeze.

I had a sudden urge to be in the sea, nearer the lifeboat, so threading my way through the tanned, glistening bodies, I found a space on the beach, quickly slipped out of my clothes and into the warm lapping waves. I was a strong swimmer and was soon creaming through the crystal water, away from the busy beach. I loved the feel of the sea, as it flowed gently over my receptive body and my mind slipped away from the world around me.

Being blissfully unaware of how long and how far I had been swimming, I rolled leisurely on my back and immediately heard the sound of a hull cleaving through the water. Shocked into consciousness of my surroundings, I could see a white sailing boat bearing down on me, and only by gulping in a deep breath and diving down into the green depths, could I avoid being hit. Looking up at the mirror surface above, I could see the knife-edged keel pass only a few feet clear of my head.

With bursting lungs, I drove myself up towards the surface and breaking into the sunlight with a gasp, I saw a white hull keel over in the wind and head out to sea. It took me a few seconds to orientate myself, when I thought I heard shouting. Shaking my head to clear my ears and treading water, I turned around in a circle and saw to my amazement the *Ukraina*'s lifeboat merely yards away, still pitching in the foaming wake.

I must have been almost upon it when the sailboat came between us. The crew were as surprised as me, to see, what must have appeared, like a mermaid launching herself from the sea, where there had been nothing moments before. Feeling completely taken aback, as I had certainly not intended to swim out to the lifeboat, I could only assume that they had come considerably nearer the shore, whilst I had been swimming in my dream world. They shouted again and I heard the sound of at least two men diving into the sea, their brown arms forging a path to my side. I tried to indicate that I was all right to my would-be rescuers, but I realised that they had no idea who I was. I found myself once more that day looking into the brown eyes of Gennadi Potenko, disbelief written all over his handsome face.

The lifeboat came alongside and we grabbed the lifelines hooked around the hull, all laughing in astonishment as the identity of the mermaid became known to everyone. Before I could object, I felt myself being firmly gripped from above and pulled up into the boat, Gennadi and his friend grasping my knees and ankles and pushing me over the bulwark into a cradle of waiting arms. Only then did I discover that I was indeed rather shaken, despite my protestations, and was not averse to resting awhile.

The rescuers had climbed aboard and Gennadi made his way to my side, gently laying a towel round my shoulders and sitting down opposite me, still disbelieving, judging by his expression. Everyone began speaking at once and to those with a little English, I explained what had occurred. They immediately offered to take me back to the beach, but it was now quite late and as we were just off the shore near the hotel, I asked to be landed there, still planning to meet Dermot.

Convinced at last that I was not hurt, they agreed and pulled strongly for the rocky headland. The hotel was very striking seen from the sea. Row upon row of balconies five storeys high, pure white against the azure sky, each spilling a brilliant cascade of orange geraniums, fiery hibiscus and delicate honeysuckle. Beautiful gardens had been created, shady trees planted, and a very attractive, meandering swimming pool was situated just above the beach.

We sailed in as close as we dared without grounding and Gennadi, understanding my intentions from my sign language and smattering of Russian, instantly leapt overboard and stood on the sandy bottom. The sea came up to his thighs and he held out his arms, indicating he would carry me ashore. Such an offer was too tempting to refuse. With encouraging comments from his companions, my heart began to pound madly, as I slipped over the side and allowed myself to be held against his warm, hair-covered chest. Holding my towel above the water with one hand, I draped my free arm around Gennadi's strong, muscular shoulders, relaxing my body against his and delighting to be so intimately close, if only for a minute or two.

As he waded through the water, there was an air of unreality about the whole experience and I longed to linger over every second. His eyes never left mine and I felt them burning into my whole being, making me tremble with giddy pleasure and I'm sure we were both thinking how this was all predestined and our lives from that moment were beginning anew. All too quickly, we reached the shallows. He lowered me slowly and gently onto the soft sand, unwilling to let go and sever the brief physical connection we were so tantalisingly allowed. We continued to stand there immobile, our eyes holding onto each other's, a smile still on both our lips, whilst the hot sun beat down on our bodies and the warm waves lapped at our feet.

A shout from the lifeboat broke the spell and Gennadi stepped back reluctantly with a whispered, '*Dasvidaniya*, Louisa,' before he turned and strode back into the sea. I stood firmly rooted to the spot, staring after him. Then raising a hand as if in a dream, I called to the crew in the boat bobbing on the sparkling water, '*Spaseeba, spaseeba*,' and began to walk up the little path from the beach to the hotel grounds.

Brushing aside a curtain of trailing mimosa, I entered a paved terrace surrounding the enormous swimming pool. It was now lunchtime and figures were dotted all around eating and drinking from a sumptuous buffet that was on display. I had tied my towel sarong-like round my body and blended perfectly with the chic clientele, as I approached the bridge which joined the picturesque little islands within the pool area.

It was then I spotted Dermot, glass in hand. He was perched on a barstool, looking relaxed and enjoying the ambience, when he glimpsed me heading in his direction.

'Very nice, darling, very nice indeed and spot on time. Where did you spring from?'

I sighed contentedly. 'From the sea, Dermot, from the sea,' and taking the scarlet hibiscus decorating the edge of the glass, I tucked it into my hair and accepted the rum punch he offered me.

7

Bridge Visits

After two more days in the Canaries that we spent eating, calling home and catching up on developing passengers' personal films, we had a sea day and a morning of bridge visits. These were undertaken by Dermot's colleague, Vladimir, due to his proficient language and social skills.

The groups were restricted to eight people at a time and spread over the course of the morning. Dermot and I took it in turns to accompany each one. We were in the darkroom after breakfast, preparing for the day.

'What happens if you meet Mikhail on the bridge, Lou? You know he's still got a crush on you.'

'I know, Dermot, I can handle Mischa. He means no harm and I actually don't mind chatting to him. He's so polite and well-educated and seems to have a whole range of English literature on board, which he is keen to discuss.'

'That is clear, Lou, and I certainly can't help there. My reading skills are not of the best but what about all that "unrequited love" business he was going on about last time? He wasn't just referring to the works of Thomas Hardy.'

'Look Dermot,' I said with a sigh, 'I like Mischa and I enjoy his company. This won't change now that I have met

Gennadi. Mischa is an officer of rank and it is a real privilege that he is permitted to socialise with us, up to a point. I never had any romantic ideas about him, as I am sure you know,' I added purposefully.

He looked doubtful, but smiled, as I gathered my equipment and prepared to leave to join the first group in the main foyer.

On my way upstairs, I was reminded how Mischa had first caught my attention. He had lingered at the bar after the captain's cocktail party and I was ordering a drink, before beginning the dining room shots.

'Good evening, Louisa. May I say how pleasant it is to have a female photographer on board. Most of the other officers have also remarked on it.' He sipped on his drink and continued staring at me.

'Thank you,' I replied, feeling slightly awkward. I had never really taken much notice of this quiet, dark-haired, unobtrusive officer before and certainly had no idea of his beautiful English.

'I wonder if you like reading?' he continued. 'I think perhaps you do, if my assumption is correct.' He looked expectant and his mouth twitched slightly at the corners, suggesting a hint of a smile.

I sipped my drink and returned his gaze, noticing how his eyes were very Slavically almond-shaped. 'Yes, I do, very much. I managed to bring several books with me to enjoy in my free time. I gather you read a lot too, judging by your excellent English. The classics?'

His eyes lit up and his smile widened, showing a row of even, white teeth. He then proceeded to reel off a list of all the well-known English literature he had read over the years.

Since that evening, we had chatted quite freely and publicly at the bar, or occasionally, on the bridge. He was the *Ukraina*'s chief navigator and this high ranking meant his privileges were fairly flexible. He would turn to me with a serious expression on his pale face and ask me to give an opinion on his latest author's work. He greatly admired Dickens with his wonderful descriptions of Victorian characters and scenes, the Bronte sisters' passion and social criticism of the times as well as D. H. Lawrence and H. G. Wells. I had read all of these authors at school and after, but Mischa would always return to one particular favourite, Thomas Hardy, who happened to be mine too.

I had been instructed to read 'Tess of the d'Urbervilles' for my A-level course and I was instantly gripped by Hardy's style, featuring romantic, tragic characters against a background of scenic beauty. Many of these relationships involved complicated love triangles, crossing social boundaries, with fate directing each person's course, right to the end. Since then, I had read almost all of Hardy's novels and much of his poetry. My favourite book being 'Far from the Madding Crowd.'

So, here began Mischa's obsession with unrequited love. His sensuous lips would draw long and slowly on his cigarette, whilst his sad eyes held mine, with a look of personal rejection deep within. I feigned not to notice and babbled on, about how the heroine usually ended up with the most suitable male character in the end.

I had never been quite sure of Mischa's real feelings for me, until one night, on leaving the darkroom in the early hours, he stepped out casually from behind a pillar, startling me briefly.

'Good evening, Louisa. I was just thinking of you. Perhaps a drink in the Kalinka Bar? I would very much appreciate your company.' His formal manner and polite, confident suggestion was attractive and I didn't hesitate to reply.

'Yes, Mischa. I would be happy to join you for a while. I need to unwind a little before retiring.' He loved this formal exchange, and his delicate mouth broke into the tiniest of smiles, transforming the usual pensive expression he preferred to display in public.

I didn't know how far Mischa was prepared to go regarding our friendship. He had been married, he told me that evening, but they were now divorced and there had been no children. Not once did he try to touch me, or get too close, but his eyes expressed all his deepest feelings, leaving me with no doubts about his affection. I really had no desire to encourage these subtle advances. I did not find him physically attractive, but there was a fragile vulnerability about him, and I felt it cruel to dismiss his attention entirely. He referred many times to 'unrequited love' and how he considered it an unfair tragedy in life.

So, our friendship remained on an even keel, never progressing beyond a platonic one. Therefore, the day of the bridge visits did not bother me in the least. I stepped out onto the immaculately, clean and functional green carpet and surveyed the peaceful scene before me. The wonderful panoramic views of the calm, blue ocean dominated my vision, miles of which remained unoccupied by any other vessel, so it appeared to me. Then, focusing on the foreground, a lone officer looked up from the radar equipment and waved me over.

'Look, Louisa. We have several ships travelling on the same course today, but we are by far the fastest, at twenty knots,' he exclaimed proudly.

He was right. I could see the tell-tale dots on the screen that indicated ships nearby, but on looking up, they could not be detected with the naked eye. Another object did attract my attention, however, and I realised this figure was very familiar. He was standing on the starboard exterior platform, surveying the horizon with a pair of binoculars, seemingly unaware of my presence. Then, glancing quickly in my direction, he beckoned me nearer, until I was so close I could smell his aftershave.

'What are you looking at, Mischa?' I said with genuine curiosity, endeavouring to focus on the area he was scrutinising.

'Oh, nothing in particular, Louisa, I just wanted to attract your attention before you got busy with your photographs,' he replied mischievously. I laughed, as he turned to face me before depositing the binoculars on a ledge nearby.

'I have missed you and our chats,' he continued. 'It's been too long since we discussed the world of fiction. You always seem so busy lately and in much demand.' His sad eyes held mine as he waited for a reply. Did he know about my visit to the crew quarters and meeting Gennadi? Was he disappointed that I had broken the rules, or jealous that I had not chosen him instead? He waited patiently whilst I debated my answer.

'I'm sorry, Mischa. There has been a lot of work this cruise and I never seem to have time to read at night lately. I'm so tired,' I replied truthfully.

He looked amused and his eyes bored into mine. 'I understand, but I am still searching for the antidote for unrequited love. I thought you might be able to help me with this problem.' He continued watching me with a hint of a smile on his lips.

'I think the only solution is to accept the situation as it is,' I replied, 'and simply enjoy a friendship and the moments spent with the person in question. That way, the pain might lessen with time.'

'Succinctly put, Louisa. I think you are very wise and also very experienced. We will talk later.' He indicated the first passenger arriving on the bridge, before he headed down to the lower deck and disappeared below.

Feeling a little guilty, but satisfied with my response, I began taking candid shots of the guests as they gathered around the navigational instruments, their faces displaying deep concentration as they listened to Vladimir's technical explanations. Then, finally, each visitor was invited to stand at the helm for several seconds, complete with officer's cap, as I captured the moment on film. This produced much hilarity. The more outgoing guests happily queued for their photos, whilst the shy ones made a hasty escape from the bridge.

8

Paradise Island

Madeira. A tiny volcanic island in the middle of the Atlantic Ocean with stunning landscapes, rugged mountains, spectacular cliffs and lush vegetation. Blessed with an abundance of fruit trees and a profusion of exotic, colourful flowers amongst which, the tropical Bird of Paradise, was most prominent. Madeira has always attracted a particular type of traveller. Ever since the island was claimed by the Portuguese in the 15th century and the land cultivated for wine and sugar cane, a steady stream of traders, merchants, aristocrats and royalty have visited this unique and sought-after destination; with the prestigious Reid's Palace Hotel being the most renowned and popular place to stay.

I stood on deck as we approached the harbour of Funchal, taking in the picturesque scene spreading out before me. The traditional white houses with red-tiled, terracotta rooftops, set amidst green verdant foliage, tumbling down to the bay where freight ships, yachts and brightly coloured fishing boats, mingled with ocean liners. This important port had been a stopping point for adventurers, expeditions and traders since the 16th century, many on their way to the Americas and the Far East.

The sun was shining, though still low in the sky at this early hour but there were misty clouds, high over the mountain tops, indicating cooler temperatures above. This reminded me of Madeira's famous micro-climate, where the weather can change within a short space of time or distance. I must remember to take a jumper with me to Monte, I told myself, as I made my way down to the main deck to join Dermot for this morning's shoot.

'All set, darling?' said Dermot brightly, as he stood chatting to an officer at the gangway entrance, camera in hand and bag slung over his shoulder.

'Of course, Dermot. We've docked perfectly today, right way round and far enough from the buses to get some great shots.'

'Excellent, Lou. Let's get ready to dive off first.'

I hurried to my cabin to fetch a jumper and camera bag; as soon as the gangway was lowered and the immigration officers had cleared the ship, the tannoy announced that the shore excursion was about to begin.

Clattering down the gangway and walking briskly towards the parked buses, we stationed ourselves a little ahead of the ship's bow, with cameras poised ready to capture the excited faces of our guests, ready for a busy day in Funchal. This shot was stunning and very popular as the background scene showed a majestic *Ukraina* dominating the landscape, surrounded by Madeira's steep, green hills against a misty, blue sky.

I left Dermot to finish off the stragglers and dashed to catch one of the departing buses, shouting, 'See you for lunch as usual.'

'Look forward to it, Lou. Have fun in Monte.'

I jumped aboard and settled down, as the tour guide's soft voice flowed over me and my thoughts inevitably focused on Gennadi. Would he be allowed ashore today? I wasn't sure how often it was permitted for the Russian crew to have shore leave, but I would certainly keep a sharp eye out for any groups of them I saw about the town. Some would be shopping as usual but not for duty free, electrical items as in the Canaries. Here, the popular souvenirs were local produce, such as the famous Madeira wine or beautifully embroidered lace creations and knitwear. Many of these were all handmade by the local women in their own homes.

Most importantly of all, the crew would be taking an abundance of photographs of each other, standing in front of famous landmarks and exotic scenery, for the benefit of their families back home. They would seldom stray from the centre of town but sometimes I had seen them outside Reid's, proudly posing before the impressive entrance to this five-star luxury establishment, overlooking the harbour.

I remember hearing that the hotel had been founded by a Scotsman called William Reid who had run away to sea, aged fourteen, and became a prosperous wine merchant. He started to build his dream hotel on the cliff but sadly died before it was finished. However, his sons finished what William himself could not and it soon became famous throughout the world.

The bus was currently travelling through the town, where staff from the cafes and bars were setting out their menus for the day, locals heading to work and housewives doing their daily shopping. Many of the old streets were narrow with smooth cobbles and I often wondered how the elegant, Portuguese women managed to navigate these obstacles, without stumbling or spoiling their beautiful leather, high-heeled shoes. I had certainly learnt my lesson early on during my shore excursions and elected to wear the flat variety.

I caught sight of some ornate mosaic pavements alongside the road, which the tour guide told us were manufactured from volcanic stone. The striking blue and white traditional tiles, covering many buildings and churches we saw, were originally a Moorish idea and often depicted local scenes or bible stories, adorning the church's interior.

As we made our way up the steep hill to Monte, we passed lavish green groves of fruit and vegetation. Vibrant, magenta-coloured Bougainvillea plants, climbed profusely over walls and glossy green hibiscus bushes, dotted with scarlet blooms, looked like little flames pointing towards the sky.

Finally, on reaching our destination of the 'downhill racers,' the bus stopped near the square. I joined the passengers on a tour of the old disused railway station, the Monte Palace Tropical Gardens and the church which held the tomb of Charles 1; the last Austro-Hungarian Emperor, who died here in 1922. It was chilly and the clouds were thick. I was very glad I had brought my cosy Norwegian jumper, which I now began pulling out of my camera bag and hastily jamming over my head, before making my way over to the toboggans. These wicker baskets had been used to carry freight down to the town, when a British merchant in the 19th century suggested the addition of a wicker seat to enable passengers to ride down too, instead of the usual three-mile hike. They are made of eucalyptus and wicker wood resting on two sledge-type wooden slats, greased with tallow.

'*Bom dia*,' I said to the local drivers as they stood waiting for the tour to begin. They smiled and returned my greeting as I placed myself to the side of the first racer and addressed the guests, cautiously taking their seats but managing to pose briefly for the camera. Then, they were speedily whisked off by two drivers, pulling firmly on the ropes attached to each side. I repeated this process many times, until all the occupants of my bus had disappeared down the slope and more buses arrived, to keep my camera busy and my mind intent on the job. Finally, with the approach of the last bus, on which I knew Dermot was riding, I sprinted over to the remaining bus, which was just about to turn and make its way back down to Funchal, and hopped aboard.

Sinking into a seat and stretching my legs out onto the adjoining one, I lazily gazed out of the window and let my mind wander beyond the busy schedule of this morning's shoot. The sun was trying to force its way between the clouds now and as they parted obediently to let it through, a shaft of golden sunlight shone down on the bus, bathing my face in a warm, comforting glow. Closing my eyes and relaxing against the soft headrest, I felt arms embracing me and Gennadi's handsome face close to mine as he carried me ashore from the lifeboat in Lanzarote. A shiver of pleasure ran through my body, as I strove to recall every precious moment and physical sensation of this fleeting and unexpected encounter. But that was three days ago, and I hadn't heard from him or seen him since! How could we live in such a small community and not connect somehow? Quite easily under Soviet legislation, I told myself soberly. Could I possibly arrange to meet him accidentally or ask Dermot if he would accompany me to the crew quarters again? I was rather afraid of the probable repercussions if I did. Maybe we had been reported to the staff captain already and Gennadi had had a warning to stay away from me.

The bus was slowing, and collecting my belongings, I got ready to leave.

'*Obrigada*,' I said cheerfully to the driver.

'*De nada*,' he replied with a grin.

I found myself close to the marketplace and I could hear the bustle of a busy day of trading well underway. A flash of red attracted my attention and I headed towards the famous lady flower sellers, dressed in colourful costumes, as flamboyant as the blooms themselves. The most popular flower, being the distinctive Bird of Paradise (*Strelitzia*) plant, which had become a symbol of the island; resembling the purple and pink beak of the bird, topped with a brilliant, spiky 'crest' of vibrant orange.

I had a little time on my hands, so I decided to wander through the market stalls and maybe take back some fresh, tropical fruit to eat in the cabin. Quickly spotting a brilliant display of fruit and vegetables, all laid out with precision and artistry, I singled out some rosy-coloured mangos, my all-time favourite, and knew I could not resist. Stuffing them into my spacious camera bag, I looked up and immediately caught sight of a group of our crew, trying on some cosy-looking Madeiran knitwear at a clothing stall. I waved and smiled as I recognised Sasha from the bar and he grinned back, sporting a locally made woollen hat with added earflaps and a pompom. I gave him the thumbs-up sign, then amidst the throng of tourists and locals cramming the aisles, I saw another face, a little further away but oh so familiar— Gennadi!

I caught my breath as he looked in my direction, his eyes locking onto mine and breaking into a beaming smile, he swiftly vanished out of sight. I hurried over towards a group of Russians, my heart thudding in my chest, scanning the sea of faces around me. But all I could see were crowds of people eagerly about their business, the atmosphere buzzing, as the energetic hawkers noisily plied their wares, and my hopes were seemingly dashed.

Without warning, a warm hand gently enfolded mine and, briefly startled, I spun around to meet a pair of dark brown eyes very close to mine. Gennadi's expression was jubilant as he took in my look of astonishment and a surge of excitement coursed through my whole body, as I squeezed his hand nervously, letting mine linger willingly in his firm, possessive grasp. He rapidly surveyed our immediate surroundings and I noticed how smoothly shaven he appeared, especially around the neat moustache and sculpted sideburns, which were tinged with a few stray grey hairs. Then, returning his attention to me, he quickly thrust his other hand forward in which he held two stunning *Strelitzia* flowers and said in Russian, 'For you, Louisa. I have missed you!'

'*Bolshoi Spaseeba,* Gennadi. *Ochen krasivah,*' I replied breathlessly. Then he was gone, instantly engulfed in a surge of tourists and I knew it was futile to search for him, as his time ashore would be short and his fellow crew companions vigilant.

Clasping the flowers tightly and tingling with pleasure, tinged with danger, I left the market in a state of dreaminess, making my way instinctively towards the harbour. Taking a detour to the right and up a hill, with which I was very familiar, I saw the entrance to a small and secluded restaurant overlooking the bay. There was Dermot seated at a table laid for two, drinking a local beer.

'Hello darling. Nice flowers! Ready for lunch? I'm ravenous!'

Smiling broadly and dropping into the chair beside him, my excitement could be contained no longer. 'Dermot, you'll never guess! I met Gennadi in the market and he gave me these!' I laid the *Strelitzias* carefully on the table. He looked surprised but seemed pleased to see me so happy.

'Lovely, Lou. The Russians are a very romantic race. It's in their genes, you know. They can't help it,' he remarked with an unusual air of sobriety.

The waiter arrived with a jolly greeting. '*Bom dia. Como estas?*'

'*Muito bem, obrigada*,' I replied happily.

'Are you having the usual?' he asked.

I looked at Dermot, who nodded in agreement. 'Oh, yes,' I replied enthusiastically, 'your prawns are the best we've ever tasted.'

Looking decidedly pleased to hear this, the waiter promptly disappeared, returning shortly with a tray of fresh, crispy bread, garlic butter, an artistically arranged mixed salad and a glass of Vino Verde for me.

Dermot and I chatted about this morning's tour and shared stories about certain passengers; particularly the interesting characters who stood out from the rest, with their lively sense of humour or flamboyant style of dress. Some of our female American cruisers liked to don sequined shoes and huge fancy hats when going ashore, whilst one gent preferred a crisp white suit with white shoes and a Panama hat. Very debonair but rather impractical when shooting downhill on a toboggan in the early-morning mist.

Our ship carried such a mixture of nationalities from northern Europe to the Americas, with most willing to integrate and make the effort to communicate. The majority clearly possessed an urge to travel, with a view to learn and discover new places and cultures. But much to our amusement, there was always a small handful of guests who looked distinctly unimpressed with everything, and obviously wished they were back home or somewhere else—but certainly not here!

The main course arrived with a flourish and two large plates of king prawns, in a delicious tomato and garlic sauce, were placed in front of us. '*Bon appétit*,' exclaimed the waiter. We ate with relish and always got thoroughly messy as we peeled the prawns and dipped the crusty bread into the thick, garlicky sauce.

Feeling satiated and relaxed, we sat back and enjoyed the warm sun, finishing our meal with milky coffees and sweet liqueurs and promising to return when next we docked in Funchal.

Making our way leisurely back to the *Ukraina*, the *Strelitzia* flowers attracting smiles and comments from passers-by, I asked tentatively, 'Dermot, what do you think are the chances of me meeting up with Gennadi next shore leave?' Adding quickly, 'I would be discreet, of course, and not expect too much.'

Dermot sighed and I instantly knew I should have kept these thoughts to myself. 'Look darling,' he said softly, putting an arm around me, 'Gennadi would be risking more than his job if he was discovered pursuing this relationship. I know how you feel but really Lou, things could get pretty sticky, not just for him but for you too.'

I knew he was right, but my former buoyant mood was rather dampened, and we walked in silence for a few minutes, whilst I contemplated his wise but disappointing advice.

Before long, we began chatting again about many things and laughing at Dermot's corny jokes and ridiculous impersonations of mutual friends—a tactic he always knew would work well, when wanting to distract my attention or lift my spirits.

Soon the *Ukraina*'s gangway came within sight and we climbed aboard, feeling rejuvenated and ready to tackle the remainder of the day's work in the darkroom and prepare for an evening of selling, as was required of busy cruise ship photographers.

9

Soon

'Dermot, are you going to dress as a British bobby or an ape this cruise?'

I was rummaging in the costume cupboard and that evening was fancy dress night. As Gibraltar was on our itinerary this cruise, we were getting the passengers in the mood. Dermot would stand outside the dining room in suitable costume attire, and I would get the shots as the guests posed with him, before they made their way to the Music Salon for the big parade later on.

'I think I'll try the ape this time, darling. I don't think I can keep that cheesy smile on my face all evening. At least, being an ape has an advantage, even though it's pretty hot in there.'

I laughed and was glad that this particular costume was far too big for me. Dermot would much rather be behind the camera than inside a ridiculous, stuffy monkey suit. I was looking forward to tonight. I knew many passengers had been busy planning their outfits all day and we were in for a fun evening. Gennadi, of course, rarely left my mind and I wondered when I would be able to catch a glimpse or even speak to him again. A thought struck me—I could request the help of an electrician to solve a problem with one of the printers in the darkroom.

'But darling,' said Dermot, 'you know there is more than one electrician on board and the chances that Gennadi would be assigned to the job are remote. We're more likely to get that old bloke with the baggy trousers we see regularly, patrolling the corridors, replacing all the dud lightbulbs.'

He was right, not surprisingly, and I smiled at this remark. Dermot was not only a realist but could usually find the funny side to most situations, which made him a light-hearted and agreeable companion. The sudden, loud ringing of the darkroom phone interrupted our chat and as Dermot was standing right beside it, he lifted the receiver. A conversation ensued, during which I gathered that our services were needed this afternoon.

'Well, who was it?' I asked, still searching for the ape costume, deep in the fancy dress cupboard.

'The staff captain,' he replied in a serious tone. 'They're doing one of those Soviet morale-boosting efforts. They need us to photograph some members of the crew, who have been particularly good workers lately. They've got a board in the crew mess where they'll be displayed, apparently.'

I almost fell out of the cupboard, tripping over a polar bear outfit in my haste, to ask which one of us had been requested by the stern-looking staff captain. His role was to monitor both Russian crew (about 300) and European staff (of which there were 20) and ensure that none of us was overstepping the political or social borders, which had been fixed by the shipping company and, ultimately, by the superior political authorities.

I faced Dermot with obvious excitement on my face and he was smiling.

'Yes, Lou. Get your camera ready. You'll rendezvous in a corner of the Music Salon, whilst the passengers are still having lunch—2pm sharp,' he said, looking at his watch. 'You've got an hour. Good luck.'

'Thanks Dermot,' I said eagerly. 'I know it's a lot to hope for but if Gennadi's there—'

'Just be careful, Lou,' he interrupted. 'Stay calm and, most of all, discreet.'

A surge of renewed energy coursed through me and as I loaded my camera and made sure I had enough spare films, I told myself this was just a routine job and Gennadi would quite possibly, not even be there. Even so, my heart was throbbing, as I entered the main lounge an hour later and saw a few crew members had already arrived, sitting quietly on the banquette seats alongside the windows. The staff captain, otherwise known to us as the commissar, was also there and he greeted me cordially, asking where I would like the crew to sit for their portraits. I chose a plain background of a claret-coloured curtain, hanging on one side of the dance floor and grabbing a chair from the stage for the sitters, I began my task.

Some of the crew knew me well, cabin stewardesses, bar staff or waiters and were very relaxed in front of the camera, since they were well used to having their pictures taken by the passengers, as well as by myself or Dermot. The Russians loved photographs and some would have a whole stack to take home to Odessa to show their families, who were eager to share a little of the exciting life outside the Soviet Union.

Dermot and I used to swap photos for bottles of Russian *shampanskoye* (champagne) or caviar with the bar staff and I was getting very partial to caviar and boiled egg sandwiches when I needed a snack in between, or instead of, dining room meals. The food provided by the Russian cooks in the galley was adequate but sometimes rather unimaginative and the repetitive menus the European staff members were used to having each cruise would seem monotonous and tiresome. We all looked forward to meals ashore, when time allowed, and many of us frequented the same restaurants, being warmly welcomed by local waiters and chefs who were always glad to see us.

One meal Dermot and I always enjoyed on board was the captain's Farewell Dinner, which consisted of a traditional Russian hors d'oeuvre or *zakuska*, such as a cocotte of creamy mushrooms and a *borsch* or *solyanka* soup. This was followed by an entree of either Chicken Kiev, fillet steak or trout accompanied by a selection of vegetables. But the highlight of the dinner, and proudly carried aloft on a silver salver by each waiter or waitress, was a baked Alaska; a mound of sweet meringue, encasing a centre of vanilla ice-cream and set alight with the addition of sparklers. The lights in the room were dimmed and the passengers watched in rapt delight, as the crew paraded through the dining room, followed by a small band playing Russian folkloric music on *balalaikas*, drums and tambourine, the sparklers hissing and raining stars atop the snowy confection. How lucky we were then, though we didn't think anything of it at the time. Certain things on board were readily available, others were not!

Now, I was encouraging them to smile, as each crew member took their place in front of me for the regulatory portrait. A familiar voice instantly penetrated my concentration and a figure seated himself directly opposite my pointed camera.

'*Zdrastvuytie*, Louisa,' said a smiling Gennadi. He was dressed in a crisp dark blue, short-sleeved shirt with white trim and open at the neck, showing some curly black hair atop a tanned chest.

I felt myself flush and asked, '*kak dela*?,' endeavouring to savour each second, my eyes feasting on Gennadi's captivating face.

'*Ochen charasho*,' he replied, looking deep into my eyes.

I returned his intense gaze, then nervously adjusting my camera, took a few shots, desperately searching for something else to say. One of the crew members behind me said something in Russian and his colleagues laughed, including Gennadi. I guessed they were telling him not to sit there all day, as there was work to be done.

All too quickly, Gennadi got up to leave and as I turned, reluctant to lose sight of him, he hesitated and whispered quietly '*vskora*' (soon), before joining his crewmates and melting quickly into the crowd behind.

That evening went well, and we got some terrific shots with Dermot's ape costume and at the spectacular turnout for the costume parade that followed. The highlight of the show was a male guest dressed as a Moroccan, in kaftan and fez, who entered the salon from the main doors and proceeded to make his way up the aisle, offering a dazzling selection of beautiful rugs to the seated audience. Following closely behind were eight of his wives, all clothed in glittering sequined robes, head-dresses with veils and gorgeous sparkling, curly-toed slippers which we had seen for sale in the *souk*. A really original idea and a well-deserved first prize, as the audience whole-heartedly agreed.

Feeling tired but pleased with the results of the evening, Dermot and I parted company—he for a nightcap in the late bar and me to my bunk, with a recently printed copy of Gennadi's smiling portrait. I wondered, with heightened anticipation, what kind of plans Gennadi had in mind and how 'soon' he would manage to fulfil them.

10

Encounter on the Rock

The early-morning sun shone like a spotlight, on the famous chunk of white Jurassic limestone that formed the Rock of Gibraltar. Standing resolute and proud and towering over the Spanish towns of La Linea and Algeciras, this small British dependency held a fascination for travellers and historians worldwide. As one historian put it, 'One of the most densely fought-over places in Europe.'

I was standing on the portside of the *Ukraina* as she reduced her speed in preparation to enter the harbour, when something bright caught my eye as it flashed by. A sleek, shiny grey body leapt again from the sea, curving above the ship's wake and trailing a fan of glittering spray from its tail. A bottle-nosed dolphin! More appeared and I watched entranced, as they performed enthusiastically for the appreciative people on the ship's decks.

The dolphins accompanied us right up to the harbour entrance and then our attention was drawn to the massive rock itself—a huge expanse of green foliage for the most part, with pretty brightly coloured houses nestling at the base, together with the medieval Moorish castle flying the Union Jack.

The passengers were keen to capture the scene and their cameras were clicking madly, as was mine, when I began touring the decks to photograph them in front of this unique backdrop. With three rolls of film in my pocket, I headed down to the gangway to meet Dermot, who was also on the Gib tour today—always very popular and solidly booked this cruise.

'Morning darling,' he said, as he stood leaning against the reception desk, talking to a pretty female assistant purser.

'How did the deck shots go?'

'Wonderful,' I replied, 'and we had the dolphins following us again, which put them all in an even better mood. I've got three rolls!'

'Brilliant, Lou. Ready for the Gib tour?' He looked at me keenly and knew I would rather be staying onboard, in case I caught a glimpse of Gennadi, or he risked some electrical job in the region of the darkroom.

'Of course, Dermot. I love the Gib trip and I want to get some new shots of the apes—they've got more babies this month.'

He smiled and looked relieved. It was far too difficult to cover the shots with one photographer and he knew that many of the passengers would expect us to be around, to ensure they received the best choice of photos possible. In truth, I was reluctant to leave the ship today, away from Gennadi but it was always more dangerous when it was so quiet on board. I would be more easily observed, so it was probably just as well. I did love Gibraltar and all it had to offer and at the end of the tour, I would meet Dermot for a drink on the Wisteria Terrace of the famous Rock Hotel. Here we could relax and enjoy the beautiful views of the Alameda gardens and the Spanish coast.

Our first stop was the Moorish castle followed by the Great Siege Tunnels. The panoramic views from here were fabulous. On a clear day, we could see all La Linea and the hills of Andalucía beyond, not to mention a direct view of Gibraltar airport with one of the shortest runways ever built. Sometimes a plane would be landing or taking off as we watched, which always caused a stir and more memorable photographs.

I found some shade and sipped at my water bottle, whilst I waited for my people to return from the tunnels. These had been excavated during the Great Siege of 1779–83, when Gibraltar had held out against the Spanish and French armies. They contained many cannon and life-size effigies of soldiers, which helped bring history to life for the avid tourists.

I turned to look eastwards towards Algeciras and saw the *Ukraina*'s bright funnel, outlined against the blue waters of the bay and my thoughts drifted to Gennadi. How he had captured my heart! I longed to be with him again but as Dermot kept reminding me, I had to think about Gennadi's position and the risks he would have to take.

My reverie was broken by the guide calling my name and we were off to visit St Michael's Cave and the apes at the top of the rock—the highlight of today's tour. As the minibus made its way down the busy narrow road into town, I watched the bustling life of Gib flash by. This small town was a melting pot of nationalities and religions. Here one could find Catholics, Protestants, Muslims, Jews and Hindus living and working side by side conversing in English, Spanish or Llanito—Gibraltar's own unique language.

What a history this place had! I could sense the past embracing me as I gazed at the medieval city walls, the huge gateways with solid studded doors, the old churches, synagogues, statues and countless cannon. The streets had delightful names such as 'Prince Edward's Rd,' 'Engineer Lane,' 'Horse Barrack Lane,' 'Cornwall's Parade' and many more; all having evolved from a particular character or trade in Gibraltar's past.

Leaving the walled city and slowing down as we passed Nelson's statue for more memorable photos, we approached the impressive cable car system. I remember the first time I travelled to the top of the Rock. It took just six minutes incorporating breathtaking views as we ascended above the Rock Hotel, reaching a final height of about four hundred metres, to be rewarded with the sight of two great continents—Africa and Europe.

Our present tour hurried on. We had no time to join the long queues already forming to board the next cable car trip. I thought I caught a glimpse of some crew members I recognised, as they gathered near the ticket booth. Pressing my face against the bus window, I tried to peer closer, but our driver sped on, past the Alameda gardens and on up Europa Road towards the Upper Rock. The houses grew fewer as we approached Windmill Hill and ascending even higher, we proceeded to enter the green expanse of the nature reserve and the habitat of the Macaques. As the driver chatted, we passed the Jewish cemetery and Pillars of Hercules and I prepared my camera for the low lighting of the next stop, where we would soon come to a halt outside the famous St Michael's Cave.

Our arrival was immediately noted, and barely before the first passenger had left the bus, we were confronted by the imposing figure of a large male ape. There were cries of delight and excitement as he nimbly leapt onto the roof of our bus and sat staring down haughtily, much to the amazement of his spectators, whose cameras were tirelessly working overtime.

Grabbing my own camera, I made my way through the gift shop to the cave's entrance. The scene that greeted me was just as spectacular as the very first time I had seen it. I stopped to take in the whole ambience of this underground spectacle. Surrounding a huge central space of the excavated cave itself, were myriads of limestone stalactites hanging from the roof in groups of varying size; all seeming to stretch their tips to meet the stalagmites growing in the opposite direction. Many meandering stairways and steps led the visitor through passages of colourfully lit limestone formations, making the visitor gasp in awe at this natural phenomenon. Every so often, during the year, there would be a live performance by an orchestra, pianist or singer within the main central cave area. This had been converted into an underground theatre—the acoustics of which were excellent. I hadn't managed to catch one of these spectacular performances yet, as our stay in Gib had never been long enough but it was certainly on my list for a future visit.

My camera was busy as usual, my people expecting the best shots I could possibly produce. After a while, I climbed one of the stairways to the biggest stalagmite of them all, joining a few other admirers at the rail surrounding it. A hand brushed my arm, and I turned in the dim light, immediately catching my breath. My eyes were focused on Gennadi's

71

radiant face, amidst the melee of tourists. He pointed to a stairway nearby, then disappeared rapidly into the gloom. The space where he had been was instantly filled by a stranger and I looked around desperately, my heart racing. Was my imagination running wild? My thoughts had been so strongly concentrated on Gennadi all morning and now here he was— or was he?

Seeing the steps I thought he had indicated, I made my way eagerly towards them, my eyes trying to accustom themselves to the increasingly low light. Taking hold of the adjoining rail tightly, my pulse pounding loudly in my head, I began to make the ascent. Each step I took became slower and more hesitant, as the surroundings darkened and I feared I might fall, until finally I found myself on an even platform. Taking one more step, I turned into an alcove and immediately felt a strong arm engulfing my waist. A thrill of anxious excitement swept over me, and I felt my body pressed up against an equally taut figure and whispering my name, Gennadi's soft, eager mouth fell upon mine. My senses soared and I could taste and smell his intoxicating scent, inviting me to meld into the contours of his warm and sensuous body, his moustache brushing my cheek, as he held me tighter and my body willingly responding. Unable to believe how this could actually be happening, the adrenaline surged through me, and I could not resist kissing him back with equal passion. My arms wrapped tightly around his waist, pulling him ever closer, our mouths eagerly exploring each other's, till a recklessness threatened to overcome us both.

Suddenly, the camera in my hand began to slip and with a jolt, I was instantly brought back to reality and the circumstances in which I found myself. I drew back abruptly and only just managed to grip the handle of the flashgun tightly, before the whole thing went crashing to the cave's floor, the result of which would, without doubt, have advertised our presence.

I felt Gennadi tense and wondered how long we had been in this dark corner. Hearing the sound of voices below, I whispered in broken Russian that I had to go as he was in great danger. He was reluctant to release me but my fear for him overcame my desire to stay. I kissed him one more time, this time with tender affection, then turned to descend the steps, my legs shaking, as I cautiously felt my way down to join my group below.

Although the cave was still full, I couldn't see my people, but a familiar copper-coloured head bobbed above the crowd.

'Well, Lou, fancy bumping into you! How's it going? You look a bit flushed!'

Dermot had arrived with his tour and immediately knew something had happened. I leant closer.

'Gennadi's here and...'

'Don't tell me, Lou. I gather you spent some time with him amidst the stalactites!' He looked at me enquiringly and not waiting for an answer said, 'Your tour is just leaving the gift shop. Better hurry, darling! See you at the hotel.'

I hastily climbed the steps leading out of the cave and reached the bus in time to head to our main stop—the top of the Rock. Gazing out of the window, my mind was filled with Gennadi and the wonderfully exciting but increasingly dangerous situation that was progressing much faster than I had intended. What we both wanted was clear, but should I let him risk his career for a relationship with a girl from the West?

My mind was in a whirl. I was battling with two conflicting messages; one of common sense and reason, against the other, a much more powerful sensation, of a highly aroused, emotionally and physically, stimulated condition. I took a deep breath to calm myself and decided to concentrate on my work for now. This was not the time to dwell on my personal affairs. My job must come first at the moment.

The bus was slowing down and there were loud exclamations as the Barbary apes came into view, a whole troupe of them sitting on the wall overlooking the harbour, with the *Ukraina* in the background—what a sight! There were many families with young, and as our group gathered round the guide, the Macaques proceeded to entertain as usual and posed with some of the more intrepid passengers. One even sat on the driver's shoulders as he spoke its name and fed it an orange. He knew them all, of course, and the new-born babies were a delight to watch. In the protective arms of their mothers, they clung tightly, as she groomed and fed the little creatures, so human-like and fascinating to behold.

One lady passenger made the mistake of opening a packet of crisps quite unexpectedly, the noise of which attracted a mischievous male ape, who fixed her with his little bright eyes. As quick as a flash, he leapt with expert agility on to the wall beside her and snatched the bag from her grasp, making her squeal before he ran off to a safe distance, followed by a group of neighbouring apes, eager to join him in this unexpected feast. Everyone was laughing, even the poor lady who had recovered her composure and was complaining that she was still incredibly hungry.

Heading back down to the town and turning southwards, a final stop at Europa Point and the lighthouse completed the tour. With a handful of films to develop, I left the bus in town and walked the short distance to the Rock Hotel, to meet Dermot and relax with a welcome glass of wine and an important decision to make.

11

Unexpected Visitors

Late that night, after the evening's entertainment of party games had worn out the happy passengers and sent them gratefully to their cabins, I was lying on my bunk, not yet undressed, going over the events of the day and reliving every precious moment in the cave. I was longing to be with Gennadi again soon and my emotions had been in such a turmoil, that I had actually asked Dermot if he could convey a message to Gennadi, through one of his crew connections.

We had been sitting in Dermot's cabin after work and I was enjoying my current favourite thirst-quencher, a Screwdriver, otherwise known to the Russians as a vodka/orange. An informative American tourist had recently told me that it had been his compatriots who had invented the cocktail in the Persian Gulf; the oil workers, whilst lacking a spoon with which to stir the drink, had used a screwdriver instead.

'Too risky, darling,' Dermot had replied seriously. 'There are so many informers amongst the crew, I don't know which ones are party members or not, let alone if they are trustworthy. It's one thing having a jolly drink with them and another to pass on interesting information which might prove fatal for Gennadi. I'm afraid you'll have to leave it up to him to make the next move, Lou. He will know exactly how far he can go and whom he can trust.'

Dermot still visited the crew quarters on occasions, but he insisted I didn't accompany him now. A far cry from that night in the late bar, when he had persuaded me to have some fun.

'The commissar quite probably knows about our little jaunt together down there by now, Lou,' he'd said soberly, 'and he's decided to overlook it, provided it doesn't happen again.'

Dermot and I had had quite a deep discussion at the Rock Hotel, away from prying eyes, and he was reluctant to encourage me further in this illicit affair. Not only could it be disastrous for Gennadi but also for me and our company in England. I also realised, to my instant dismay and shamefulness, that the plans Dermot and Katya had painstakingly made over the last year or so could quite possibly be jeopardised, if another wayward photographer was found breaking the rules. This thought brought home to me just how focused I had been on my own happiness, without proper regard for either Gennadi or my dear friends. I, therefore, resolved to try and immerse myself in my work and not think constantly of Gennadi and when I would see him next. What will be, will be!

I picked up a Russian-language book and tried to focus on some new vocabulary I thought might be useful for conversing with the crew—be it Gennadi or otherwise. Deep in study, my concentration was broken by a gentle knock on the door and half-expecting Dermot, I called, 'It's open, come in.' After a moment's hesitation, the door opened slowly and first the blond head of Gennadi's friend peered around, then, as he proceeded to enter the cabin, he was followed by Gennadi himself—a bottle of Russian champagne and a plate of appetisers in his hands.

I sat up in shocked amazement, hardly believing my eyes. I never dreamt Gennadi would risk visiting my cabin again—and with company. For two members of the crew to be here was unbelievably dangerous and obviously only possible because their quarters were so near mine.

Closing the door swiftly behind them, they stood smiling and looking slightly embarrassed till, finally getting control of myself, I asked them in Russian to sit down. As there was only one chair in the room, Gennadi's friend quickly made himself comfortable and I gestured to Gennadi, as I shifted further up, that he could sit at the end of my bunk. As he did, his eyes locked onto mine and feeling a rush of excitement, I was back in the cave, he was pulling me close and we were kissing with a passion that we could not control.

I was brought back to the present when I heard the blond sailor speaking. He introduced himself as Nikolai and in a mixture of Russian and English told me that they had been planning to visit me for some time, but the opportunity had not arisen. Then after this morning's events, Gennadi had decided he must see me soon and Nikolai had provided moral support.

It now became apparent that Gennadi had planned a supper for two and Nikolai stood up to leave. Instantly, I panicked. What if Dermot, or another member of staff, came to my cabin on some pretext? More importantly, how could I physically resist Gennadi if left alone with him? Things were moving too fast. I quickly found three glasses and asked

Nikolai to pour the champagne. With a glance at Gennadi, who nodded agreement, he did as I wished, and we toasted each other and drank, as my pulse raced and my heart pounded.

Anxious to seem at ease, though inwardly in a turmoil, I tried to avoid Gennadi's arresting dark eyes, which were constantly fixed upon mine, but it was impossible, and we continued to gaze at one another whilst our limited conversation slowly ebbed away.

The champagne had a relaxing effect, and with the bottle almost empty and my visitors plainly comfortable, I eased my previously tense body a little on the pillow. Being so delightfully close to Gennadi, I could feel the heat of his body and smell the soap on his skin, as he leant a little closer to place his empty glass on the table next to mine. I wondered if his thoughts were echoing mine. How long could we continue like this?

I was aching to throw myself into his arms and taste the sweetness of his kiss once more, but my desire was immediately tainted with anxiety, as a vision of Katya and Dermot flashed before me, their future resting on my subsequent actions. As long as Nikolai stayed here, nothing physical would happen between Gennadi and me. We would all have an enjoyable evening and hopefully none of our superiors would be any wiser.

Desperately trying to convince myself to do the right thing, my confusion must have been apparent as Gennadi looked concerned and asked me if I was happy that they had come.

'Oh yes, Gennadi,' I replied without hesitation. 'Of course. But I am worried that we will be found out.'

'Don't worry, Louisa,' he said softly as he took my hand in his and turning it palm upwards, put it to his lips. I trembled with pleasure and unable to resist any longer, all other thoughts fled my mind. He pulled me close, so close, I could feel his heart beating wildly against my own.

'*Ya tebya lublyu,*' he whispered, looking intensely into my eyes with a passion so sincere I was lost in another place, another time, where only we two existed. In a remote part of my mind, I heard the soft click of the cabin door as Nikolai, knowing that he was no longer needed, quietly slipped away and left us alone together, at last.

Then Gennadi, gently but firmly, took me in his arms and as I looked up into his face, full of adoration, I knew that he was at that moment the most important person in my world. Softly, he kissed the curls on my forehead, my ear, my throbbing neck and finally my parted lips. My heart no longer pounded but beat strongly and evenly against his chest in eager anticipation.

12

The Black Ship

Another sea day was upon us, and Dermot and I prepared for a full day of selling in the shop before the evening's entertainment. We had taken some beautiful photos of our passengers visiting the Alhambra yesterday—a World Heritage Site and a marvel of the Moorish occupation. The palace/fortress was built in the mid-13th century and the many beautiful gardens, pools, fountains and stunning architecture, provided a host of colourful and photogenic backgrounds for our enthusiastic visitors.

Dermot and I had worked late in the darkroom that evening, managing to print off about half the films we had taken, and it wasn't until 2.30am that we both decided to call it a night. My heart raced as I made my way back to the cabin, imagining a repeat of the night before, when Gennadi and I had at last been alone together and our fervent loving had determined the path we were, unavoidably, to follow. But as I undressed and fell into bed, I knew that any future nights we spent together could not be predetermined. The danger was far too great for Gennadi, and I reluctantly reminded myself to be grateful to be able to see him at all.

So now, after a good night's sleep and feeling refreshed, I was catching up with the processing and printing of passenger personal films and listening to a new cassette I'd bought in a Spanish music shop, featuring one of my favourite singers at the time, Billy Joel. I turned the volume up, because I knew the solid metal door of the darkroom would mute the music and not bother anyone who happened to pass by. I danced happily to the infectious beat whilst trimming each small print from its neighbour, on the long roll which had been drying on lines stretched across the lab. Then the tempo changed and a slow, romantic track came on and I imagined dancing in the arms of Gennadi, on a dance floor somewhere, just the two of us and no one around to break the spell.

So immersed was I in my own world, I hardly noticed the change in the ship's engines, until the music ended and the cassette player clicked to a gradual stop, waiting for the tape to be turned over. I stopped trimming and listened intently, as the vibrations decreased and the engines slowed dramatically—like they did sometimes in mid-ocean when the crew were instructed to perform a man-overboard drill. But this felt different. The ship wasn't turning as it would in normal circumstances. I decided to investigate.

I collected my camera, as was my habit, and hurried up several flights of stairs to the boat deck along with some guests, who were curious to see what was going on. The familiar humming noise of a boat being lowered on the portside, drew me and my companions towards the sound. Unsure of what I would see, I stepped out onto the boat deck. My mind was certainly not prepared for the huge apparition towering above my head. Its massive bulk eclipsing the sun and casting a shadow over the full length of the deck, making me shiver with an ominous sense of foreboding.

A large black ship, bigger than the *Ukraina*, stood bobbing in the sea before me. Another Soviet vessel with a hull so large, I just stared in awe at the sheer size. I saw a hammer and sickle painted on the funnel like ours and screwing up my eyes, I could read the name emblazoned near the bow—*Anton Chekhov*. My instincts told me that something very unusual was about to take place.

My intuition proved to be correct, as I peered over the railing and saw the lifeboat stop a few feet from the surface of the water, near the crew deck, where the lower gangway was situated. The door there was already open and I saw an officer looking out. Shortly after, a fair-haired, male crew member appeared out of uniform and stepped into the lifeboat. My heart sank as I suddenly realised what was happening. For some reason, the boat was transferring crew from the *Ukraina* to the black ship and both Russian ships were travelling in opposite directions. This could mean that the other ship was heading back to its home port, Odessa. Panic instantly gripped me, as another male crew member boarded the small boat and I thought of Gennadi. If he and I had been found out, could he also be one of those unlucky people leaving the *Ukraina*?

My stomach began to tie itself in knots as I pressed harder against the rail, craning my neck in an attempt to see who would emerge from the doorway below. Surely, we had been discreet enough? Gennadi would never risk anything he was unsure about, especially with the solid advice and responsible attitude of his longest and closest friend, Nikolai.

There was a pause, then a shout, as the officer called to someone inside the ship. A third person materialised, wearing jeans and with very dark hair. I could only see the back of his head and I prayed it wasn't Gennadi. Please not this way—we would never see each other again!

As soon as he embarked, the boat was lowered into the water and immediately cast off. I was desperate to see his face and reassure myself that Gennadi was still on board. Please turn around, look up! Then as the engine revved and the boat began to turn away from the *Ukraina*, the black ship veered slightly in the wind allowing the sun to shine down on the small boat as it made the short journey to the other side.

At the same time, the dark-haired man tilted his head towards me as if looking for someone, whilst my heart thumped like mad and my eyes strained, as I leant further over the rail to see his face. He shouted something and his gaze changed to someone on the deck below me and I breathed a sigh of relief. It was the bartender from the late bar, saying his farewells to a friend still on board.

'What's all the hullaballoo, darling?' said Dermot casually, as he approached from behind and leant on the railing beside me. 'Oh, it's the *Chekhov*! I'd forgotten how massive she was. Worked on her once, ages ago.' He didn't need me to explain, as he quickly assessed the scene. 'I wonder where the poor sods are going?'

'Maybe Odessa?' I suggested worriedly.

'Yes, possibly. Maybe stepped out of line. I can't imagine that great hulk over there needs three of our crew members. Anyway, look, they're climbing aboard now and our lifeboat's heading back. Show's over, Lou. Let's get back to work and make a bob or two.'

He turned to go, then quickly turned back and said quietly, 'Lou, that was thoughtless of me not to realise. You must have been scared out of your wits. "You know who" could have been one of those on the boat.'

'Yes, Dermot, that thought had crossed my mind,' I replied curtly, 'and I was just getting over the trauma when you appeared.'

He put his arm around me. 'I'm sorry, darling. Forgive me. Let's go and get a drink at the bar.'

'All right, Dermot,' I said, smiling, 'I think I need one to steady my nerves.'

13

Danger Lies Ahead

Looking back, I could hardly remember all the events of the days that followed. After entering the Mediterranean Sea and leaving Malaga, the ship was due to head north to Valencia and Barcelona, before the final destination, Genoa.

I went about my work with great enthusiasm and vigour, accompanying the passengers on shore excursions and being on hand aboard ship to cover all the daily events for the eager and appreciative guests. But the days meant nothing to me, I lived for the nights. The warm moonlit nights, when in the small hours, Gennadi would come to my cabin.

After Malaga, I had the pleasure of enjoying his company every night, or at least part of the night, due to Gennadi's increased confidence that he would not be detected. However much Nikolai advised against these regular illegal visits, Gennadi's determination would always prevail. So, Nikolai offered to act as a lookout, to help reduce the chances of discovery.

I remembered lines from a poem read in my school days and now expressing my feelings perfectly:

And knowing that what is now about to be

will all have been in oh, so short a space.

I never saw him in the daytime, even though I searched the faces of any crewmen who came on deck. I would almost despair of seeing him and then the soft knock would come on the cabin door, and I would quickly run to open it, lest he should be seen waiting outside. His handsome face would be smiling, as he rushed to hold me in his arms, pressing my body tightly against his own, as he covered me with hungry kisses.

We would make love beautifully, tenderness escalating to passion and moments of great ecstatic unity. I knew that I was in the grip of emotions I had never thought possible, and I felt joyously fulfilled, but also slightly vulnerable. The future was light years away and only occasionally, would my mind dwell on the difficulties and complications that would, almost definitely, lie ahead for us.

No one else knew of our affair, except Nikolai. Even Dermot seemed unaware of the frequency of our meetings, and I was still concerned that, if we were ever discovered, he might be implicated somehow. I therefore deemed it wise not to divulge too much, but even so, he must have sensed a contented glow about me. On more than one occasion, I caught him studying me and about to say something, then, quickly changing his mind and smiling, turned away shaking his head.

The second time Gennadi visited my cabin did indeed take place on the evening of the crew transfer to the *Chekhov* in mid-ocean. My face must have displayed a look of profound relief when I hurried to close and lock the door, as soon as he stepped over the threshold. We kissed wildly and frantically and clung tightly to each other for a few moments, before I managed to breath the words. 'The *Anton Chekhov*, Gennadi. I was so scared!'

His face relaxed. 'Yes, *dorogaya*. There was talk in the crew mess of the ships meeting the night before, and I decided to delay my visit to you. It was very difficult, Louisa but safer for both of us.'

I wholeheartedly agreed and asked why the three crew members had left the *Ukraina*. We were now sitting on my bunk, arms around each other and he told me what he knew. One of the men had to return to his home as there had been a death in the family, and Sergei, from the Kalinka Bar, had been overheard disclosing too many personal affairs with an American passenger. The third man had apparently been caught trying to separate himself from his two colleagues, whilst ashore, on more than one occasion.

'I feel sorry for all of them, Gennadi. It could so easily have been you!' I replied passionately, hugging him again.

'I know,' he said, softly. 'But here I am, *dorogaya*, and all is well.'

He drew me closer, and we kissed deeper and harder this time, eventually falling back onto the bed, bodies entwined, desire burning fiercely, until we were soon lying wonderfully naked and thoughts of danger very far from our minds.

The morning was fresh and fragrant and the sky a powder-blue as I boarded the tour bus in beautiful Valencia. We were soon preparing to disembark at the first stop—the attractive art nouveau building of the busy railway station, decorated with stunning tiles and magnificent mosaics. Then, we walked next door to the huge bullring, strikingly impressive against a clear Spanish sky, creating a favourable backdrop for my first compositions.

I was feeling buoyant and contented, knowing that I could expect to see Gennadi at the end of the day, and the frustration of the past ebbed enormously as I prepared to devote my attentions to the morning ahead. This tour was as hectic as usual, and you had to be fairly fit to complete it. Most of the time was spent following the guide through the narrow winding streets of the old city, stopping here and there in a *plaza*, or heritage site of interest, for a brief historical explanation. We passed several beautiful churches and palaces, busy restaurants and cafes, many surrounding large fountains; their waterjets sparkling in the sun and sometimes delicately spraying us if we happened to get too close.

Dermot and I had split up, as usual, to capture as many of our guests as possible, whilst they roamed this ancient city of Neoclassical, Baroque and Gothic architectural wonders.

I looked up and caught sight of *The Miguelete,* the tall octagonal tower of the cathedral, whose 207 steps some of us would now climb. The views from the top were spectacular and my people were glad to pose for me against a teeming background of the Queen's Square, the blue-domed churches and the fertile land of the *huertas* (agricultural land) beyond.

Descending again, and quietly entering the confines of the cathedral itself through an adjacent door, I could sense the suppressed excitement of our group. We were now approaching an adjoining chapel, which housed a very special ancient relic. With soft murmurings and a respectful tread, we prepared ourselves for what we were about to see.

Here, in this sacred and peaceful location, protected within a glass casket was, what was deemed to be, the Holy Grail; the chalice Jesus was said to have used at the Last Supper. Joseph of Arimathea had also used it to collect Jesus's blood as it dripped from the cross. We took our seats in the surrounding pews and gazed in wonder, feeling overwhelmed, as the silence intensified, broken only by a few muted sighs. The cup was actually quite difficult to see clearly, due to its small size, the lighting used, and the distance from our seating area; it was situated in an alcove behind the altar. The guide had told us that the original object had been very plain, but gold handles and a base had been added at a later date, together with a variety of jewels.

I now adjusted my camera and set the exposure for a slow shutter speed, flashguns being forbidden here, and was confident that the ambient light would help me obtain a soft, glowing representation of the chalice for later sales on board. Resting my forearms firmly on the pew in front, my zoom lens extended, I was at last able to see the holy relic; the brown agate upper part of the cup, supported by a decorative base with handles, shining with assorted jewels. I held my breath whilst I gently squeezed the button and took a few shots.

After a short stop at the little cathedral shop for important souvenirs, we all emerged from the cool of the building into the warm, sunlit bustle of the busy square. I purchased a refreshing *horchata* (tiger nut milk) from a kiosk, whilst waiting for our group to gather. Then heads were carefully counted, before marching off in the direction of the central market. This was a photographic delight, and with many colourful local produce on display, our passengers strolled past the stalls sampling fresh fruit, willingly offered by the vendors and inevitably making more purchases. I stocked up on my supply of *turron* (nougat) and Valor chocolate and popped them into my camera bag for later; a lovely treat when working late into the night, when something sweet was needed to keep me awake.

The tour was now nearly over, and I heard the guide informing our group that thirty minutes would be given to wander the square before returning to the ship. Some people looked delighted and rushed off to claim a seat in a nearby cafe, gratefully resting their tired feet whilst sipping a cool drink. Others seemed slightly apprehensive and preferred to linger close by the guide, in case they lost sight of her and their only way back to the safety of the ship.

I had arranged to meet Dermot at a cafe in a side street, and quickly taking leave of our friendly guide, I left to weave my way through the throng of tourists that had now entered this popular part of the city. Glancing back, I couldn't help smiling as I noticed our more timid guests move ever nearer the guide, until she was totally surrounded and unable to move from the spot.

Retracing my steps, I proceeded towards the Plaza de La Virgin, taking careful note of landmarks on the way. Many times in the past, I had taken the wrong turning and ended up back at the marketplace again—totally disorientated. Very soon, I recognised a small museum entrance and headed to the right, down an even narrower alleyway. There were fewer people around, and much to my relief, I immediately saw the cafe's familiar bright sunshades in a row, under one of which sat Dermot, chatting with the French singer from the ship. They were laughing when they noticed my arrival and Dermot waved cheerfully, whilst removing his glasses and wiping his eyes, saying. 'Hello darling. Wait till you hear what happened last night! It'll be all over the ship by now. Tell her, Dani.'

I was intrigued and curious to know what had caused such hilarity, and I couldn't help giggling myself—their mood was so infectious. I quickly ordered a drink from the hovering waiter and sat down to join them.

Danielle was a glamourous blonde French vocalist, who wore slinky sequin dresses and had a voice like Edith Piaf. I prepared to hear some celebrity gossip, as she directed her lovely blue eyes towards me, took a sip of wine and began the story in her strongly accented English.

'I was sitting at the bar in the Kalinka, late last night, enjoying a drink with the other entertainers, when the staff captain arrived and offered to buy me a bottle of champagne. He had seen the show that evening and thought my performance was exceptional. I could not very well refuse, and much to my regret, he directed me to a secluded corner of the club.' She raised her eyebrows and pursed her lips before continuing, 'Well, after about half an hour of tedious conversation, I was searching for an excuse to leave, when I realised he was a bit tiddly and would not let me go easily. I looked towards the bar and saw Mario, the Italian shop man, who had noticed my predicament and, with a sympathetic nod, slipped off his stool and promptly left the bar. I had hoped he would somehow come to my rescue and glancing around at the few remaining passengers, I decided I had to risk the staff captain's displeasure and call it a night.'

At this point, Danielle started to laugh again but composing herself quickly, resumed her narrative. 'Suddenly, there was much laughter and loud exclamations from the passengers and crew, and all our eyes turned towards the bar's windows.' These were small porthole-shaped windows surrounding the centre of the bar itself, and the view through them showed part of the pool on the deck above. Normally all we saw, amidst the clear blue water, would be a few legs and feet of the swimmers themselves. But tonight, the scene was very different. Danielle was staring with unbelieving eyes at the solitary male swimmer, who had discarded his trunks and was making his way slowly past each small window, enabling all the spectators to get a clear view of his private parts.

'We were all glued to the windows,' said Danielle, 'and could not believe what we were seeing, when an enraged staff captain leapt out of his seat, his face showing deep disapproval, and hastily left the bar. It was then that I made my retreat to my cabin and knew I would owe Mario a debt of thanks in the morning for his unusual diversion. I sincerely hoped he had disappeared from the scene of the crime in time.'

'Well, had he?' I asked tentatively.

'Yes!' She replied happily, clapping her hands. 'He is a born practical joker! Even if the staff captain suspects Mario, he has nothing to prove it was him.'

The story had certainly travelled the length and breadth of the ship by the time we got back after lunch. And late that night, I was laughing again (albeit discreetly) with Gennadi, as we shared the details of this event and I revealed the true reason for it taking place.

The ship had a day at sea after Barcelona and was then due to call at Genoa. I longed to be near Gennadi again and my mind was fully focused on the approaching evening, when he would undoubtedly appear in my cabin.

I was later than usual in retiring, as the passengers had enjoyed a particularly hilarious passenger talent show with a record number of entrants. No one could have guessed we had so many accomplished singers, dancers and comedians amongst our cruising guests. They really were very entertaining. As Dermot and I worked to capture their performances on film, each shooting at different angles on either side of the lounge, we were suddenly surprised by the appearance of a flamboyant magician in top hat and tails, who was the star of the show.

The cameras went crazy and people gasped with delight as he proceeded to produce a large bouquet of flowers from his jacket and vanish a passenger's cigarette in the palm of his hand—only to make it reappear behind another guest's ear! Even the ship's resident entertainers applauded enthusiastically, along with everyone else, as the contestants all lined up on stage for a final bow.

It was very late by the time Dermot and I finished in the darkroom, and although we were both quite tired, we were very satisfied with the evening's work. We strolled along the passageway, Dermot's arm lightly around my waist, my high-heeled shoes swinging from my hand.

'Shall we break open a bottle then, Lou?' Dermot asked as we approached his cabin door.

Looking at my watch, I realised that if Gennadi came that night, it would be soon, so I shook my head, unwilling to offend my friend and said, 'I think I've had enough tonight, Dermot. I'd rather turn in—another evening perhaps.'

He glanced at me and looked as if he knew perfectly well what I was thinking. 'You're quite right, darling, bed it is. Sleep well.'

He kissed my cheek before we parted, and I walked the few yards further on to open my cabin door. Flicking on the light, I caught my breath, as Gennadi stepped out from behind the door and we fell into each other's arms.

There seemed a strange intensity in his lovemaking that night and later I lay awake, my head cradled in his arm, observing his peaceful features as he slept. His hair so dark and soft, his long lashes, a neat Slavic nose leading to a full and sensitive mouth, above which he wore a long-clipped moustache. How much longer could we go on meeting secretly like this? What would happen when we got to Odessa? Did he really love me—enough to declare it to everyone—and how would they react? After all, Dermot and Katya were to be married soon, so it *was* possible. I sighed and closed my eyes, holding Gennadi a little closer, trying not to let the future spoil the present.

I must have dozed for several minutes, when a sudden noise alerted me to danger and my eyes flew open instantly. I could hear loud, purposeful footsteps coming along the corridor, nearer and nearer until finally stopping outside my cabin door. My heart was pounding and my body tense as I sat bolt upright and Gennadi, awake by this time, put his finger to his lips and we both froze. A determined fist knocked loudly.

'Open this door, Louisa, at once!' a Russian voice said, speaking good English. A voice I knew, belonging to the chief purser—a moody man I had never liked.

Gennadi's face had turned as pale as wax, anger showing in his expression. As he looked at me, I saw a glimpse of fear in his eyes, but his strong arms holding me proved the fear was not for himself, but for me.

It came again, the knocking, but louder now. 'Open up immediately. I know you are both in there.'

Gennadi swung his legs quickly and quietly to the floor, picked up his pile of clothes and silently crossed the room to the corner behind the door, where only a few hours earlier he had hidden and surprised me. He signalled to me to go and open it, when the knock sounded a third time, much louder, accompanied by the door handle being tested.

'All right, all right, I'm coming—wait a minute,' I cried. Dragging the sheet from the bunk, I wound it around my body and pointed urgently to the wardrobe. Gennadi, now dressed, slipped noiselessly inside and vanished out of sight.

I pretended to have difficulty unlocking the door, then slowly pulling it towards me, I let in a crack of light. Instantly, a powerful body forced me back and slammed the door wide open against the wall. Two men entered and the chief purser started to shout, 'Where is he? We know you have a lover in here. Tell us, or we'll search the cabin!' A hot wave of anger swept over me and I became strong and unafraid.

'Get out of my cabin!' I said in a raised voice. 'You have no right to burst in here. Get out at once!'

The officers looked surprised and for a moment, the younger one hesitated, but the chief purser was determined. In a voice low and menacing, his red face close to mine, he said, 'You have been watched. It has been reported you have visits from one of the crew and it is forbidden, as you are no doubt aware. We have little jurisdiction over you, but we can discipline him.' Then he snarled at his junior in Russian, 'Search!'

I sprang forward but the big man was quick and forced me back against the wall, holding my arm in a vice-like grip. The younger officer did not take long to find Gennadi, and he emerged, white-faced and defiant to stand before the chief purser. There was an exchange in rapid Russian, short staccato answers by Gennadi, before he was pushed roughly past me to the corridor outside, glancing quickly in my direction as he was hurried away. I was left facing the cold, expressionless face of his captor across the chaos of my cabin—the bed in disarray and the wardrobe door still swinging open.

'The captain wishes to see you. Get dressed and come with me at once,' the chief purser demanded.

'Very well,' I replied in as curt a voice as I could muster.

'I will wait for you outside. Be quick,' he barked.

I pushed the door shut with such force, it just missed catching his hand as he exited. Turning the lock quickly, I leant against the wall, breathing hard, my heart thumping. This sequence of shattering events had only taken about ten minutes, but I felt as if I was in another world, another place. My fingers holding the sheet around my body were cramped and sore, my feet cold and I began to tremble all over. I couldn't think straight but I knew I must get dressed and go quickly to the captain, to ensure I did not earn more disfavour.

My discarded clothes of the happy evening in the Music Salon lay over a chair, and I hastily pulled on my cream trousers and black short-sleeved blouse, glanced in the mirror and pinched a little colour into my dead white cheeks. My head was filled with the one thought that I must, at all costs, take the blame for the relationship. I must absolve Gennadi of any of it—even if it meant losing my job.

Holding my head high, I opened the cabin door and walked resolutely up the corridor, following the chief purser's rapid, impatient steps.

14

Reprisals

The captain was seated at his desk near the window, in the office section of his quarters, which was located near the bridge. He was a quiet, middle-aged, white-haired, serious-looking man. He seemed to prefer performing his duties backstage rather than lingering over his social obligations, unlike other captains I had known.

My hopes rose as, opposite him, sat a junior officer whom I recognised—a blond fresh-faced Russian with an American accent. I knew him from bridge visits, the reception desk and also as a drinking partner of Dermot's. He was a pleasant and likeable person. According to Dermot, he only got the job as a translator due to his fluency in English, which he credited to an American radio station he was able to listen to whilst at sea.

The captain, speaking in Russian, indicated that I should sit next to Vladimir, as he would be responsible for translating all that was necessary. This fact meant that it was going to be a formal occasion and the captain would only converse in Russian, even though his English was fairly good.

I decided to be open and reveal my true feelings for Gennadi and declare that none of what had happened was his fault. The situation was entirely due to my headstrong personality and I was prepared to apologise for the inappropriate actions I had made. But the captain's first words hit me like a bolt of lightning out of the blue. My prepared speech swiftly vanished from my lips, as I tried to digest all he had to say.

'What have you done, Louisa? You realise that Gennadi Potenko is happily married with a wife and young child in Odessa. This flirtation he had with you means nothing more.'

My stomach muscles tightened, I felt sick and my thoughts raced. Married, a child? It can't be! He would have told me! It must be a lie. A way to make me feel used and ashamed of my deeper feelings. A way to warn me to end the relationship. But if he did have a family, I was the one who had allowed myself to be misled. Instead of falling in love, I should have just enjoyed a fleeting affair—nothing more. My mind was filled with confusion. A mixture of despair and anger swept over me.

'No,' I whispered, 'I didn't know. I thought he loved me.'

The captain spoke again through Vladimir. 'You were wrong,' he said. 'He cares only for his family. They are waiting for him in Odessa. He has disobeyed our rules and we will decide what must be done. The chief purser will contact you soon, once a decision has been made.'

My whole body froze as I continued to stare at the captain in disbelief. He seemed unperturbed and nodded briefly to Vladimir, indicating that the meeting was over. There was nothing more to say and with a heart that was weighing me down, I glanced at Vladimir who was watching me with what appeared to be an expression of sympathy.

My eyes were stinging with suppressed tears as I stumbled back down the stairs to the deck below, only to see Gennadi making his way towards me on the other side of the rail. He looked up and his dark eyes held mine in a profoundly intense gaze, almost as if he were willing me to read his mind. As we crossed paths, he smiled reassuringly and reached out to take my hand and gave it a gentle squeeze. My heart leapt and my hopes were raised. He did love me—I felt it to be true. Whatever his marital position, I still believed he held me in his heart.

Vladimir, following in my footsteps, gently urged me on down the stairs and Gennadi was gone, as suddenly as he had appeared, and I knew where. It was his turn to be summoned to the captain's quarters, to be questioned and dealt with accordingly.

I headed straight for the darkroom, and it was here that Dermot found me, shortly after he had checked my cabin and breakfasted alone, thinking I had gone for an early-morning walk on deck, as was my custom some sea days. My face, which was almost definitely red and blotchy, together with watery, bloodshot eyes, told him all was not well. His cheerful smile faded as he asked me hesitantly if I had been the reason for the commotion in the corridor last night.

I stopped printing and turned down the music as he pulled a chair up beside me and prepared to listen. With great patience and compassion, he took in all the descriptions of events, emotions and fears I had experienced only a few hours before, remaining quite silent until I ended the story. My greatest concern now, I told him, was not for me but for Gennadi and the uncertain penalty he must now pay.

His usual bright eyes displayed a sad expression, and it would have been very easy for him to say that this turn of events was to be expected and I had brought it on myself, but being Dermot, I knew otherwise.

'Lou, darling,' he said, looking me straight in the eye, 'I am sure nothing terrible will happen to Gennadi. The only thing you can do now is to carry on working as usual and try not to worry too much. Do not try to contact him and do exactly what the Russians ask of you—it's useless to oppose them. I'll visit the crew bar later and see if I can find out what's going on. Nikolai might be there. And I'll do the shop duty today if you'd rather stay below decks,' he added thoughtfully.

I spent the rest of the day with a heart so heavy and a body so tense, I could barely force myself to consume any kind of food. Dermot tried to encourage me by bringing some snacks to the darkroom and a glass or two of vodka/orange. This helped somewhat to get me through the day, which was always a busy one with final sales and orders before the end of the cruise.

Throwing myself into a busy regime certainly helped to lift the burden of despair and I even began to hope that the commissar, who was to determine our fate, might brush the incident aside and, at the worst, forbid us to carry on with our relationship.

We had been at sea all day and were scheduled to dock in Italy tomorrow, to disembark the passengers and collect new ones for the beginning of another cruise. Dermot and I usually spent the morning in the photoshop for last-minute sales and then saw to the accounts. Later we'd go ashore to a nice restaurant in the city and relax for a couple of hours over a tasty Italian meal, before visiting our two gay friends, Gino and Tony, who ran a local hotel, where we would drink the best cappuccinos in town.

Feeling a little stronger and more positive after the normality of the day's work, I was changing for the evening meal when the phone in my cabin rang and I was told to report to the chief purser's office immediately. My hands shook as I slowly replaced the handset and leaving the cabin, I headed for the reception area and tried to prepare myself for what the chief purser might tell me.

Would they actually punish Gennadi and how? I had heard that privileges could be withdrawn, and reprimands given. How severe they could be for Gennadi, I did not know. But from newspaper reports in the West, many people had been sent far away—some even to Siberia! I began to panic. I had to help him. Maybe Dermot would know how.

I knocked on the purser's office door, my heart thudding so loudly, I barely heard the abrupt response to enter and sit down. The chief purser was at his desk and looking up, smiled with an air of satisfaction, making me feel distinctly uneasy, as was his intention. He said in a cold, detached voice, without the slightest hesitation, 'You will leave the ship tomorrow in Genoa. It has been arranged. You will not return. Do you understand?'

This was an outcome I had not envisaged and my stunned countenance, patently obvious, was keenly observed. My brittle defences, now instantly shattered, caused involuntary tears to flood my eyes and the vision of my tormentor, still smirking, blurred and distorted horribly before me. But my mind continued to think rationally and I asked, in as strong a voice as I could summon, 'What will happen to Gennadi? Can I see him before I go…please?'

Another malicious grin crossed his face, as if he knew I would request this final meeting. 'He will disembark in Odessa in a month's time. You can see him now but only for a few minutes, and you will not be alone. Vladimir will accompany you.'

Five minutes later, I entered a cabin in the officers' quarters, where Gennadi was sitting looking serious and pale, and I longed to hold and comfort him and tell him that everything would be all right. I sat down next to him and Vladimir took the seat opposite.

I barely knew where to begin until Gennadi started to speak in Russian, in a cool and distant manner, hands clasped tightly together and averting his eyes when they happened to rest on me for a moment, whilst Vladimir slowly translated. He seemed altogether indifferent and unconcerned as he acknowledged the existence of a wife and daughter in Odessa, whom he loved and said he was sorry not to have told me at the beginning of our affair. Our affair! After all we had been to each other—all we had shared! This was not the Gennadi I had grown to adore more than anyone else and embraced with all my heart and soul.

My raw emotions were plunged into turmoil at his dismissive and casual attitude. I felt cheated and used. How could I have misjudged him? He glanced at me again and I knew he saw profound sorrow and confusion in my face, and it seemed to me that a sudden hopelessness appeared in his eyes, as if he were pleading with me.

Was all he had just told me the truth? Why would he lie? Surely it wasn't the fact that Vladimir was there, who was obviously uncomfortable with the situation and was willing to translate anything Gennadi and I wished to say to one another. Vladimir was known to prefer socialising in the crew mess rather than spending time with his fellow officers, and everyone felt at ease in his company. But as Dermot kept telling me, 'No one is trustworthy, darling, even the ones you least suspect.'

Coming to my senses, I realised there was more that Gennadi wished to say but he had been forbidden to reveal it. Surely, his superiors had instructed him to say these hurtful things. The political officers on board would probably not tolerate another Russian breaking their rules with a wayward photographer—Dermot's case had been difficult enough to deal with.

Though loathe to leave Gennadi's side, I felt defeated, drained and helpless. I was convinced that this meeting had been fabricated and could see that we would progress no further. I sighed and looking deep into Gennadi's forlorn eyes, said, 'I understand, Gennadi. I am very sorry for everything.' He nodded, looking slightly anxious, as Vladimir glanced at his watch, stood up and turned towards the door.

Without warning, Gennadi clutched my hand and fixed me with an impassioned expression of, what appeared to me as, determined defiance. I held onto his firm grip for as long as I could and returned his piercing gaze, endeavouring to reassure him that I was trying to understand. Hope rekindled within my aching body. This was not over, I told myself. I *would* see him again and I would do all in my power to protect him against any kind of repercussions—the severity of which I dared not imagine.

15

A Glimmer of Hope

'But Lou, I can't believe you're actually going,' cried Dermot incredulously. 'This didn't happen to me when I started seeing Katya.'

We were in my cabin later that night, after a hectic evening, covering the captain's farewell cocktail party and hastily getting the prints ready for the early-morning shop sale.

'Probably because you were the first in the company to be intimately involved with a Russian and the authorities were persuaded to come to terms with it,' I replied. 'Besides, Katya wasn't married, like Gennadi, if what he tells me is true,' I added gloomily.

Dermot was helping me pack and it wasn't easy. I seemed to have accumulated so many new things—souvenirs and clothes mostly. We crammed them into my bags and placed them outside the cabin door, to be collected by sailors and taken upstairs sometime during the night.

Physically and mentally exhausted, we collapsed on the bunk and Dermot put his arm around me and I rested my weary head on his shoulder. I felt the tears of despair would come now, if I didn't hold them back. I mustn't weaken, we had little time and too much to discuss. There was a bottle of Russian champagne on the table, which a bartender had traded for photos, and Dermot suggested opening it whilst we talked. It was refreshing and energising, and we talked and planned well into the night.

'If Gennadi isn't leaving the ship for four weeks,' I said, excitedly, 'the ship will dock again in Genoa in two weeks' time, for the repositioning cruise to Odessa. I could come back and try to see him—maybe he would be allowed ashore.'

'Don't be ridiculous, darling,' he said, quickly. 'They'll probably keep him below decks from now on and watch him like a hawk. He won't be allowed anywhere near the gangway. But,' he added as an afterthought, 'with my crew connections, I could listen in on the grapevine and try to get a message to him, saying you'll be in Genoa in a fortnight's time. At least, that's something. I could maybe help further as the go-between. I'll have to think.'

Dermot had indeed gone down to the crew bar that evening to seek out Nikolai and perhaps glean some information, but he had bumped into Vladimir instead. He had had a few vodkas and was consequently very talkative, telling Dermot that he was unhappy about his part in the Gennadi incident and hoped that the authorities would be lenient on him. He liked both Gennadi and myself and could see that our love was genuine. All Vladimir seemed to know was that Gennadi had been confined to his cabin, whilst the staff captain conversed with the authorities in Odessa. There was no rush to make an instant decision, he said, as there was a whole month till the *Ukraina* arrived in Odessa and half the cause of the problem—me—would be gone by tomorrow. My thoughts at this comment suddenly reminded me of the *Anton*

Chekhov and the transferral of three of our crew members in mid-ocean a few days ago. Nothing was certain nor impossible.

The captain's cocktail party did not provide me with a clue either, concerning the general mood of the superior officers. The captain smiled genially to each passenger as he posed for the regular end of cruise photographs, and even the commissar seemed his usual self, mixing with the guests and looking relaxed. Both of them had greeted me when I initially entered the Music Salon, and no one could have guessed there was anything amiss. Only one person deemed it necessary to remind me of my indiscretions, and that was the chief purser himself, who scowled at me whenever my glance happened to land in his direction.

I didn't get much sleep that night, knowing it was my last night aboard the *Ukraina,* and I kept frantically hoping Gennadi would somehow find a way to come to my unlocked cabin—one last time. But as the light began to filter its way through the thin curtains, shading the porthole window, I realised that dawn was breaking and the chance to be with him faded, as the sun grew stronger and the familiar shipboard sounds increased as a new day began.

Knowing that the ship had an hour to go till we docked in Genoa, I dressed hastily and hurried upstairs to the reception area. I saw with a pang my bags waiting neatly by the gangway exit door. All too soon, I would be accompanying them ashore—away from my dearest love and not sure if we would ever see each other again. I looked around the bustling crowd of passengers and crew in the foyer, scanning every person, in case Gennadi was able to get close or even send a message somehow. An arm embraced me from behind and I jumped slightly, startled; turning around, I was met with Dermot's familiar face peering down at me, filled with a mixture of sadness and deep concern.

'I'm all right, Dermot,' I said quietly. 'I'll be disembarking as soon as the last passenger has left the ship. I just hoped something would happen before I left Russian soil, but I expect it's better this way—at least from Gennadi's point of view. I don't want to make things worse for him.'

He hugged me closer and said reassuringly, 'I'll help you get to the hotel, Lou, and settled in before returning to the ship.' Then lowering his voice a little, 'There may be a message with some new information from Nikolai. Try not to worry too much.'

Meanwhile, Dermot and I manned the photoshop for an hour, which was extremely busy, with guests who had left their photo purchases till the last minute and others who had bought everything and were collecting the latest from the previous evening's shoot.

The accounts quickly taken care of, with paperwork and cash handed over to the purser's office by Dermot, it was time to say my tearful goodbyes to the other Western staff members, with whom I had worked so closely over the last few weeks. Then, with Dermot for company, I resolutely made my way down the gangway, to the familiar sights of Genoa docks. Stepping ashore and severing myself physically from Russian territory, I happened to glance up towards the bow of the ship and hesitated briefly. A familiar figure, standing on the bridge outlined against the bright sun, raised his arm and slowly waved. It was Mischa. Even though our chats had ceased and I had hardly seen him at all these past few days, he had not forgotten me. I waved back sadly and knew I would not forget him either, or the wonderful conversations we had had. I quietly wished him well and hoped he would eventually find the love he desperately needed.

A short distance from the road above the port area lay the hotel we knew and frequented every time we began or finished a contract with a shipping line. Our friends, Gino and Tony, were always there to greet us and make us comfortable for our short stay.

As soon as Dermot and I approached the hotel's entrance, we saw Gino polishing the glass doors with great enthusiasm. Looking up, he gave us a beaming smile, followed by a cheerful *ciao*, but immediately sensing something was out of place, his expression changed to one of concern. Helping us with the heavy luggage, he held the door open and ushered us inside.

Making ourselves comfortable on the brown leather sofa opposite the reception desk, Tony offered us both a cognac with our usual frothy cappuccinos, and as Gino handed over the few letters that were waiting for us, we briefly told the pair of my predicament. 'All will work out in the end, *mia cara*,' said Gino. 'Love always triumphs, you'll see,' he added encouragingly.

I smiled wanly and Dermot drained his drink, hugged me one last time and headed back to the ship. He promised to get in touch the moment he had any important information and reminded me that I must inform our boss in England about the situation as soon as possible. He would understand and be sympathetic, Dermot confidently told me. I wasn't so sure.

Half an hour later, as I lay on my bed in the hotel room, I picked up the phone to call my company, not really having any idea how my employer would react. My job would, undoubtedly, be forfeit for a while and I would probably never be allowed on a Soviet ship again. There was even the dreadful chance that my company might lose their contract with the whole of the Black Sea fleet—about fifteen vessels in all. This would be devastating but even worse, for me, would be Gennadi's likely outcome. My mind was racing again but before I could rehearse my prepared dialogue, the phone was answered by the familiar, deep and steady tones of my employer's voice.

Breaking things gently was never my forte and instead of building up to the disastrous denouement with Gennadi, involving a hierarchy of officers aboard the *Ukraina*, I launched straight into the fact that I had been thrown off the ship for getting involved with a Russian crew member. There was a short silence, as the news was being digested at the other end of the line, and I feared that the contract with the Russian liners would now indeed be teetering on the brink. But to my surprise, my employer was calm and understanding, and reacting to my shaky and uncertain tone over the phone, he said he'd deal with the outcome as before and I was not to worry. Meanwhile, he would book a flight straight back to Blighty for me tomorrow and I was to wait to hear from him.

Feeling somewhat relieved, now that part of the weight had been lifted from my wearied body, I dialled my home number and briefly related the latest turn of events to my worried parents. I assured them that I was fine and would be with them tomorrow, when I would tell them the whole story, together with my plans for the immediate future. Now, utterly drained, I fell back on the pillows and must have fallen into a deep and much-needed sleep.

It wasn't until three hours later that I woke with a start to look at my watch—it was five o'clock. Just one hour till the *Ukraina* sailed from Genoa. No time to lose. I must hurry down to the quay to see if Dermot had any news or I could somehow say farewell to Gennadi. I freshened up my face and hair and hurried down to the lobby, where Tony was watching TV whilst waiting for the next customer to arrive.

'See you soon, Tony,' I called above the noise of the film he was watching. 'Just popping down to the ship to say goodbye. Back for an early dinner.'

'Good luck, *mia cara*. I'll have my special *pasta marisco* waiting for you. *Delizioso!*' he replied, kissing his fingers in typical Italian fashion.

Walking quickly towards the docks, I wondered what news, if any, there would be from Dermot. I knew I wouldn't be permitted to board the ship and I must try to be discreet and not expect to see Gennadi, when he was probably being kept well out of sight. Easy to say, I thought. My desperate eyes would be scanning the whole of the crew deck, just in case he managed to escape temporarily.

The passengers were all aboard and the ship was preparing to leave. How I longed to join them and go about my normal duties. The ship's Italian agent was finalising the manifest documents with the chief purser near the gangway— I certainly didn't need to bump into that particular officer right now. So, I turned and headed in the direction of the stern and the crew deck, where the sailors would appear soon to prepare the ship for departure. I had watched then many times, hauling in the tough and heavily plaited ropes that secured the huge ship alongside.

A voice called from the deck above and I looked up to see Dermot smiling down, camera in hand, 'Hi darling. No news I'm afraid but I managed to get a message through. I'll keep my ear to the ground. See you in a fortnight. Have a safe flight. Got to go now.'

He gave me a jolly wave and disappeared out of sight. I knew he was trying to be tactful and not draw unnecessary attention to my presence. For that, I was grateful, but I still felt lost and frustrated and continued staring up at the deck, till I realised someone was calling my name from the starboard side of the ship.

A blond head appeared amidst the crew that had come to work the ropes, and I immediately saw the friendly face of Nikolai, Gennadi's closest ally, a few metres above. My hopes rose as he came closer to the rail, holding something in his hand. He looked casual as he leant over the side and threw it, so that the object landed close to my feet. It was a pink rose, and I knew instantly what it meant—Gennadi had not deserted me. This was a symbol of his affection, as it had been that first morning when I had found the same flower by my bedside after that fateful crew party. It seemed so long ago now.

Nikolai smiled reassuringly and turned to attend to his duties, whilst I hastily bent to pick up the rose and held it to my breast. The heaviness in my heart lightened and my resolve hardened to face whatever the Russians put in my way to reach Gennadi and to save him from the politics of Soviet Russia.

16

Back to Italy

The plane circled the coast of Genoa and my pulse raced as I strained to see out of the small window. There below, shining brightly in the morning sun, stood a large white ship docked alongside the cruise terminal—the *Ukraina* had arrived, with Gennadi still aboard, somewhere below decks. My whole heart ached for him. How was he spending his time? Was he still allowed to work on board, and did he think of me as often as my thoughts turned to him? Questions I hoped I'd find answers to, if circumstances allowed.

I had had one brief phone call from Dermot when he went ashore in Naples, assuring me that Gennadi was still on board, but he hadn't been able to contact him directly yet. I felt Dermot was being cautious and rightly so, as his personal situation was still delicate and ultimately uncertain, until he and Katya were finally wed.

I checked into the hotel and hurried down to the cruise terminal. The Genoa docks were drab, dull and unattractive, not a place to linger for pleasure, and I hurriedly made my way over the network of bridges, located under the public thoroughfare above. Approaching the customs office on the corner, I stopped abruptly, gathering my thoughts. In my hurry to see Gennadi, I realised I didn't have a proper plan, and if a ship's officer saw me and reported back, they would ensure that Gennadi was confined to crew quarters—if he hadn't been already. I peered around the corner and saw the *Ukraina* towering above me—such a familiar sight and a place I'd called home for several happy months. Some crew members were currently disembarking from the small lower gangway, many of whom I recognised. They would spend an hour or two shopping in the busy city, buying electrical items or clothes to take home to their families in Odessa. Some would also try to sell items at a profit to acquaintances, who weren't lucky enough to leave the Soviet Union but were eager to acquire Western consumer goods.

They headed in my direction in their regulated groups of three, one person in each being an official member of the communist party, instructed to keep an eye on the other two. Hardly a relaxing way to spend shore leave but it proved effective, and it was a rare occasion when a crew member mysteriously vanished in the backstreets of some foreign port, never to return to his or her homeland.

As I had lingered awhile, an Italian customs officer in his smart uniform looked up from his desk in his office piled high with documents and enquired if he could help me. My covert behaviour must have looked strangely suspicious and knowing that there had been some arrests in the docks for contraband goods, I quickly replied that I was waiting to meet a close friend from the ship. It was to be a surprise. He smiled and bent his head again to continue his work and I stepped back into the shadows, allowing the Russians to hurry past, intent on their mission, as their time ashore was short.

I decided I must make a move and strode out of my hiding place towards the crew deck, which was nearest and in the shade of the overhanging buildings of the port. I sat on a bollard and strained my eyes as I gazed up at the decks. They were deserted, as all the passengers had disembarked as soon as the ship had docked and been cleared by customs officials. Probably half the crew too had already been allowed ashore.

The sun was dazzling as it reflected off the water, making it sparkle with shimmering, silver stars and the slow rocking of the ship created little ripples round the sides, forcing the taught ropes to creak, as they pulled tightly against the bollards. How delightful to experience these familiar sights and sounds again. As the last of the disembarking crew members left the harbour, I began to relax and let the warm breeze flow over my tense body, my mind drifting off into memories of happier times. A time, not so long ago, when I was standing on the deck high above, looking down at a handsome boy in a small boat who was smiling up at me, never imagining for one moment, how he would completely change my world and that of his own.

Suddenly, the ship's tannoy system burst into action, and I was jerked out of my daydream to hear a familiar Russian announcement: '*vnimanya ekipazha*'—'attention crew members.' This was followed by a list of Russian names and a request that they report to the staff captain for a meeting immediately. No doubt a new set of instructions regarding general conduct had arrived from the Odessa authorities. This was a common occurrence, and my thoughts once again returned to Gennadi and how he would eventually be treated by these same authorities.

Feeling nervous and frustrated as I continued waiting for something to happen, I began to think that my great plan of seeing Gennadi before the ship sailed was beginning to look bleak. I must contact Dermot; he would know what to do next. I stood up, and right on cue, a welcoming voice beside me said, 'Hello, darling. You made it back then.' It was music to my ears. I turned and threw my arms round Dermot's neck and looked up into eyes expectantly.

'He's all right, Lou. The only thing is, he's confined to the ship—nothing more. Here, take this.'

He placed an envelope into my hands and looking down, I saw my name written neatly in Russian on the front.

'I'll go back on board and see if I can contact him,' said Dermot. 'Don't move from this spot.'

Before I had time to thank him, he had rushed off, his tall frame walking purposely towards the gangway and out of view. What would I have done without him? How would I have contacted Gennadi? Well, if it hadn't been for Dermot, I would never have met Gennadi in the first place and discovered emotions I never knew I had. He had been such a support and I had many reasons to be grateful to him, even though we both understood the gravity of the situation and its possible end result.

I studied the envelope again and sliding my finger under the seal, I carefully pulled out the paper inside. There were two pages of beautifully written Cyrillic script and, remembering my lessons, I began to translate the first line:

Hello Louisa,

I was very upset to hear that you had to leave the ship so suddenly.

'Louisa!' said a much-loved, familiar voice.

My heart leapt as I looked up and saw Gennadi's smiling face, only a few yards from my head. He was leaning on the rail, looking well and very pleased to see me—so maddeningly close and yet so very far out of reach. Dressed in regulation white, short-sleeved shirt and blue trousers, his hair recently washed, and his moustache trimmed, he appeared to be in good health and prepared for my arrival.

'I am so happy to see you again, Louisa,' he said in Russian. 'Thank you for returning.'

'I had to, Gennadi. I was so worried.'

My Russian-language lessons had continued in earnest during those two weeks in England, and I was able to construct some sentences now, much to Gennadi's pleasure.

He smiled reassuringly, then looked behind, and I could see Nikolai urgently beckoning to him. He turned back to me and said quickly, 'I love you very much, Louisa. I think you know that.' His face was serious and his eyes unwavering as they held onto mine.

My throat tightened and I managed a few words. 'Yes, Gennadi, I believe you. I am so sorry it ended like this.' I wanted to say more but something was holding me back. It wasn't the fact that my language skills were lacking but something else. A doubt still existed in my mind that if Gennadi did have a family to go back to, I would eventually be forgotten, no matter how much he professed to love me. I suppose it was a way of shielding myself from the pain, for ultimately, I believed, *I* would be the one to bear the deeper, emotional scars.

He put his hand on his heart and turned to go as I watched helplessly from below, desperately wishing he could stay a little longer. But he was gone. Vanishing quickly into the gloom of the inner deck, leaving me rooted to the spot, for what seemed an incredibly long time, his letter clutched in my hand; the only physical connection I had to sustain me.

Then Dermot's soft voice beside me said, 'You'd better go back to the hotel, darling, for Gennadi's sake. He risked a lot coming out on deck just now. You have his letter to translate and lots of planning to do. When you get home, you need to arrange travel to Odessa in a few weeks for the wedding—visas, flights and hotel bookings. It will all take time. Then when you arrive in Odessa, Katya will help you contact Gennadi, if that is still what you want.'

I knew he was right. He realised exactly how I was feeling and his gentle but sensible reminder stirred me into action. I looked at him with confidence, my face bright. 'Yes, Dermot, I *will* go now and get started on those details. Not a moment to lose. I'll see you in Odessa and maybe, by then, you'll have more news of Gennadi.'

We hugged and parted. He to his duties on board and me to study and translate the precious letter I carried, which would reveal, I hoped favourably, all that Gennadi needed to tell me about his secret past and what effect it would have on our possible future together.

17

The Letter

The prospect of reading Gennadi's letter was causing two opposing emotions to occupy my mind. Whatever he had to tell me would determine our path for the future. I was excited and eager to discover all he had to reveal but there was also a sense of dread that his words might disappoint, and I would be left with just wonderful memories of our brief and predestined time together.

The neat Cyrillic script blurred again as my tired eyes struggled to decipher each precious word. I had tried to translate the first paragraph in the hotel and later on the plane, but I was floundering in a sea of new Russian vocabulary and grammar as yet unknown to me. How frustrating this was, and I decided to wait till I arrived home again and had access to my Russian-language course books and my comprehensive dictionary.

Back in England, I shut myself away for the afternoon and got down to seriously translating all Gennadi had to say and rewriting it in English, to the best of my ability. It began to make sense very soon and I found that the verbs were still recognisable in their present, past or future forms—unlike some of our English ones.

Hello Louisa,

I was very upset to hear that you had to leave the ship so suddenly. I found out only after you had gone. I had hoped that we would, somehow, see each other again. I feel very guilty about my behaviour during our last meeting which, surely, is impossible to forgive.

Where are you now, Louisa? What feelings have you left for me?

During our last time together, in the presence of an interpreter, you received a terrible insult. Forgive me, but I had been forbidden to speak the truth about my true feelings for you. Surely now our separation is indeed confirmed! How bitter to acknowledge this.

I want you to understand that during our brief time together, I was always deeply in love with you right from the start. And it torments me to think that I will probably never see your eyes, your hair, your lips again. Louisa, I love you! These words come from my heart and I will cherish all the wonderful moments we were lucky to have together. I very much hope you can do the same.

When I am home, in Odessa, I will meet every passenger ship that calls in the hope that I will find you and see you, if only for a moment. Louisa, I have never felt this strongly about a girl before and I know I never will again as long as I live.

Once more, forgive me.

Kisses

Gennadi

MS Ukraina 1981

I put down the pen and wiped away my tears. The sincerity of the letter moved me and I was struck by the eloquence of his words and beautifully composed lines—what artistry and passion still existed in Russia today. No matter what the world thought of communism in general, no one could deny that most Soviets had access to a good education, some even exceeding that of their counterparts in the West.

I sat and thought about all Gennadi had told me. His true feelings were clear but what of his family ties, if any, and of his future in Odessa? I knew he would never be allowed to leave his home country again, but would he be punished further? Maybe he wasn't sure either.

He appears to believe that I would probably not wish to pursue our relationship, but he does not hesitate to say that he will continue to love and search for me still. How would I be able to find him without an address or telephone number? I had scanned the letter and envelope for a clue, but with no success. Did this mean he had something to hide? I was again plunged into confusion and wondered if following my heart was the right thing to do. Of course, it was right, I chided myself. Gennadi had opened his heart and risked his job and the right to travel, to be with me. I would regret, perhaps for the rest of my life, not to pursue every possible avenue to find him.

But one thing was certain. Dermot was getting married, and I had made up my mind to travel to Odessa to be with him on this momentous occasion. And maybe, during my short visit, I could find Gennadi, with Katya's help, and discover more about him and his personal life. And, if it were appropriate, I would tell him I was seriously in love with him and willing to do anything to ensure his safety. Perhaps then, our future together could become a reality.

18

Magnificent Moscow

Arriving at the prestigious Metropol Hotel in Moscow, I stepped out of the small taxi that had carried me from the airport and was immediately blasted by the ice-cold air that hit me with breathtaking force. It was December, after all, and although I had donned my big, grey fur coat and warm boots, my face and head were exposed to the elements and I felt the blood draining from my extremities. I had always loved wintery landscapes, especially from a photographic angle, but this was not the ideal climate for someone with circulatory problems; I could feel my fingers numbing up already under my sheepskin gloves.

The snow had stopped falling and the roads had been cleared with Soviet efficiency, together with the main pavements in this district. Hurrying quickly through the main doors of the hotel, I was met with a more agreeable temperature and art nouveau décor of a bygone age; marble walls, high ceilings and grand columns. But this Intourist hotel also had a shabby, old-fashioned, seen-better-days feel, as did many older Russian buildings from the last century. The modern Soviet touches were also apparent in some contemporary furniture, hotel signs and renovations, that were far from keeping with the original style or quality. But it was inexpensive and one of the hotels in which a foreigner was permitted to stay.

Checking in and collecting my key, I was instructed to proceed to the second floor where I would find my allocated room. Fortunately, I carried only one medium-sized bag and my smaller camera bag, as there was not a porter in sight— maybe they didn't exist here? Anyway, on exiting the antique and laborious lift, I stepped out into a badly lit foyer, where a middle-aged Russian woman sat at a large table, eyeing me with obvious, unsmiling, curiosity. She looked at my key number and pointed down the ever-darkening corridor, with the well-used patterned carpet, to where I would find my room.

I remembered from a guidebook on the USSR that these *babushkas* were employed on each floor of every large hotel, to assist the guests with any requirements—one of them being a plug for the wash basin. There seemed to be a shortage, or perhaps certain guests couldn't resist taking one home!

My room was plain but functional, and I lay on the bed and rested for an hour, whilst the night came early. I thought about tomorrow, when I would catch an Aeroflot flight to Odessa and spend four days there with Dermot, Katya and, I hoped, Gennadi. I was highly excited at the prospect of seeing him again and had decided that this was my only hope of discovering the truth. I could not rest till I had followed it through.

Meanwhile, I had arranged to meet a Yugoslavian businessman I had become acquainted with on the ship for dinner that evening. He worked in the city and had offered to show me around if I was ever in Moscow.

125

The room phone rang at 7pm and it was Stefan, saying he was in the hotel foyer and would wait for me in the bar on the ground floor. After showering and changing—no plug needed—I left my room and passed by the *babushka* in a floral head scarf, at her desk. '*Dobryi viaycher*,' I said as I headed towards the stairs, rather than taking the lift—I thought it might be quicker. She replied with the same greeting, whilst surveying me with continued interest. As I descended the staircase, I noticed, with amusement, that a pair of well-worn comfy-looking slippers were poking out from under her table.

Stefan greeted me warmly. He was the same as I remembered—tall, dark and with a smile that made the fine lines at the corners of his eyes crinkle, giving him an endearing quality. He must have been about forty, well-travelled in the Soviet satellite countries and with a very good command of English, which stood him in good stead when entertaining foreign businessmen visiting from the West.

We left the Metropol and headed towards Red Square on foot. Being in the centre of the city, there were so many famous sights within walking distance. We were passing the impressive facade of the Bolshoi Theatre and the more recent and less impressive Hotel Moskva, when Stefan turned to me with a worried look saying, 'Why didn't you bring a hat, Louisa? Everyone wears one in Russia in the winter. You'll freeze!'

'I'm fine,' I replied, looking at the brown fur hat he was sensibly wearing; the kind with flaps tied on top which could be undone to cover the ears. 'Though it certainly is colder than I have ever experienced!' I exclaimed, as my warm breath filled the air in front of my face. My fingers were stiffening again and I felt sure the blood had drained from my nose and cheeks.

We soon reached Red Square where the gold cupolas of the Kremlin shone brightly in the illuminated lights, and St Basil's Cathedral stood in all its gaudy beauty, outlined against the clear starlit sky.

'Did you know, Louisa, there is a legend saying that the two architects of St Basil's delighted the tsar so much with their creation, that he blinded them in order to prevent them from building another?' said Stefan enthusiastically.

I gazed up at the colourful onion domes and felt a deep sadness for the men whose future careers had been destroyed, by the will of a selfish tyrant. 'No, I didn't know,' I replied soberly, and the feeling of joy, which had gripped me on first seeing the church, ebbed away and I was left with a confused, uncomfortable sensation. I thought of Gennadi and his future and the punishment that could be inflicted on him, which constantly tormented me, until Stefan grabbed my arm and steered me towards the nearest metro station.

Descending below street level and entering the subterranean world of the Moscow Metro was something I was not prepared for. Having been on the London Underground on many occasions, I had envisaged a similar experience; how wrong could I be? Noticing a distinct temperature rise, due to the enclosed space and other bodies present emitting warmth, we purchased our tickets and joined the many other Muscovites, heading down on a busy escalator, descending into the deepest depths below.

I gazed around at my surroundings and was pleasantly surprised by the clean, white marble walls and ceilings, lit by huge, impressive chandeliers. No tatty adverts or litter to be seen, just tasteful elegance in an extraordinary location and commuters going about their business, in an orderly fashion. As I continued to stare in wonder and admiration at the spectacular scene, Stefan was intrigued by my expression and exclamations.

He smiled and said, 'I can see you are more than a little impressed by Joseph Stalin's creation, Louisa. *The Underground Palaces of the People* were first begun in 1935 with a combination of Art Deco and Socialist themes.'

'This is a work of art, Stefan!' I gasped. 'Something I would expect to see during the tsarist era, not a communist one.'

As we left the escalator and proceeded on foot, my eyes were dazzled by the rich ornate ceilings, the decorative arches and beautiful Russian mosaics and frescoes along the walls.

'The Russians have always regarded art and culture as being a vital part of their very existence; from the beginning of Christianity in Kiev, they believed God revealed himself to his people through the beauty of art. It was deemed a divine gift, whose essential purpose was to serve God and uplift humanity. They are very proud of their artistic heritage. Stalin wanted to reinforce and encourage this cultural tradition within the Soviet regime. He also intended to make this metro the most spectacular one in the world!'

'Absolutely mind-blowing, Stefan. I could wander here for hours on end!'

He laughed and said, 'No time, Louisa; if we want to secure a table for dinner, we must hurry.'

He guided me towards the waiting train, and on boarding, I was engulfed in a welcome stream of warm air supplied by the efficient heating system. We found seats easily amidst the evening commuters, whose snatched glances in our direction didn't go unnoticed. I smiled back and was met with either indifference or awkward curiosity. How sorry I felt for these people's controlled lives, but I suppose most of them hadn't experienced any other way and maybe felt secure within their familiar regimental world.

There was very little conversation taking place, as a great number of commuters were immersed in worn-out copies of various books. Stefan noticed my curiosity and explained quietly, 'Before the revolution, 65% of Russians were illiterate but since the Kremlin's mass education drive to stamp out illiteracy, Russian authors and poets now enjoy a larger audience—not just contemporary authors but new editions of the classics. For example, the young woman opposite is engrossed in a copy of *Anna Karenina*. The people here have a ravenous hunger for culture.'

On ascending the steps to the road, I saw that we had arrived in another part of the city and Stefan guided me towards what had once been a grand-looking building but was now rather rundown in appearance. There was a substantial queue leading up to the large wooden door of the establishment—people waiting to be assigned much desired seats in the obviously popular restaurant. This hardly surprised me. The Soviets were well used to spending a great deal of their time waiting in line for food of some sort. I steeled myself to join them, for what could be at least half an hour standing in the crisp evening air, stamping my feet and trying to conserve the warmth remaining from the metro a few minutes before.

But Stefan had other ideas, and with a slight shake of his head, he beckoned me to follow him to the start of the queue, where a well-dressed group of four waited patiently to be allowed entry, as soon as the door swung open. I felt deeply embarrassed as all eyes immediately turned towards us, and although I couldn't detect any sign of animosity, I heard someone quietly mutter the word *inostrantsy*—foreigners—as we passed by.

Stefan raised his fist and knocked firmly on the door, whereby it was pushed slightly ajar from inside and an expressionless, male face appeared in the gap. Then, to my great astonishment, Stefan proceeded to speak in English with the doorman, asking to be given a table for two as soon as one was available. Whether the doorman understood was not clear, but he nodded and the door opened just enough to let us both enter, before closing again on the other poor, long-suffering prospective clients.

Stefan looked at me and smiled as we deposited our coats in the small cloakroom, before a stocky, middle-aged waitress approached, to guide us to our table, situated in a large dining room of tsarist splendour. I marvelled at the tiled floors and ornate high ceilings with elaborate crystal chandeliers, before reaching our table alongside a wall of beautiful walnut panelling.

The table was laid with a pristine white linen tablecloth, upon which were arranged a variety of Russian beverages—Georgian red and white wine, *Moskovskaya* vodka and carbonated water. My awkwardness swiftly disappeared as Stefan poured me some wine and I began to survey the other tables in the busy dining room. Most of the clients were well-dressed, as were we. I had chosen to wear my dark blue, tailored trouser suit with a cream, silk blouse and Stefan looked suave and sophisticated in a silver-grey suit, white starched shirt and silver tie. Studying the clientele more closely, I realised that this restaurant was one of those frequented by the elite of the city—foreigners, factory managers, army generals, acclaimed writers, artists and diplomats. I had no idea that such places existed outside the hotels.

There were few women present, and the ones that were, looked like the wives of local senior party members, with their dyed blonde hair and ample frames squeezed into twin sets, in mainly muted tones. The general atmosphere increasingly relaxed as more vodka was consumed, together with the familiar Russian *shampanskoye*.

We started our meal with black caviar, sturgeon in aspic, and an array of pickled vegetables together with some traditional Russian black, rye bread. This was followed by 'Borshch Moscow Style,' with a bowl of soured cream, which I found delicious and satisfying without feeling too full to enjoy the main dish—a mound of tender strips of beef mixed with thinly sliced onions and mushrooms with a hint of mustard, in a soured cream sauce, topped with a few crispy matchstick potatoes.

I was very impressed with the quality of the Beef Stroganov and as I relayed this to Stefan, he confirmed what I already knew—that if you have the right social standing in Soviet Russia and enough financial support, you can enjoy a much better lifestyle. Rather contradictory of the original Soviet ideals introduced by the founder of Russian communism, Vladimir Ilyich Ulyanov (Lenin).

My appetite appeased, I was now content to enjoy a cup of lemon tea to round off this splendid meal. But Stefan informed me that it was not quite over yet and I was to taste a very popular dessert in Russia made with two simple ingredients—pureed apples and bread. This turned out to be a *Babka Yablochnaya* (Apple Charlotte) and it reminded me of English bread and butter pudding, but with a bit more imagination. The waitress brought us two small portions, with a bowl of apricot sauce to spoon over the top of the crusty bread exterior and a scoop of traditional Russian ice-cream to add to this sweet delight. I had tried this ice-cream before, on many Intourist ship tours, and found it particularly creamy and unlike any ice-cream I had previously tasted.

As we finished our meal with the customary tea and lemon from a bubbling samovar, a small band arrived to play on the stage opposite the diners and we listened to traditional Russian folk music, attracting many happy couples to the dance floor.

I turned to Stefan. 'It's been a lovely evening, Stefan. You really have spoilt me. Thank you so much. I have now seen another side of Moscow life I was completely unaware of.'

'I am so glad you contacted me, Louisa. If I can be of any help in the future, please let me know. I hope you find your Gennadi and things turn out the way you both want them to.'

We made our way back along the sparsely lit street, our footsteps leaving prints in the newly fallen snow. I shivered and Stefan took my arm, as we hurried to the metro and back towards the warmth of the Metropol Hotel.

My flight to Odessa in the morning was due to leave at 11am, so I hugged Stefan in the lobby and thanked him again for a memorable evening. He took my cold hands in his and wished me well, reminding me to buy a hat at the first opportunity.

'It's amazing how much warmer you will feel, Louisa,' adding with a look of concern, 'Odessa can be very cold too, so please take my advice.'

I smiled as he turned to go and I wondered if I would ever see him again, or indeed return to this grand and fascinating Russian capital.

19

Welcome to Odessa

On boarding the Aeroflot flight to Odessa, I was immediately struck by the stark appearance of the cabin furnishings, the familiar musty smell of worn-out upholstery and the lingering aroma of *papirosi* cigarettes. I appeared to be one of the few passengers on board and, on looking around, most certainly the only foreign one.

As I gazed out of the small window, the plane began to taxi amidst more falling snow and I saw to my immediate anxiety, that the runway was thick with it; surely, we couldn't take off in these hazardous conditions? Soon, I thought, we would all be told by the captain to await the clearance of the runway, to enable a safe departure.

I was to be proved wrong. Almost at once, the plane's momentum increased and we prepared for take-off. My hands gripped the arms of the seat and I held my breath. With my face glued to the window, all I could hear were the plane's thudding wheels on the encased runway and my heart almost matching the beat as we raced ever faster to reach our goal. Suddenly, the plane tilted upwards with a great effort, the snow-covered runway receded from sight, and we were at last able to make our ascent.

Relaxing my grip, I looked around and was surprised to see the other passengers with heads bent, more interested in absorbing the latest contents of Pravda than observing what was going on around them. All too familiar a procedure, I suppose, if they were regular travellers during a typical Russian winter.

After an hour's flying time, during which I had to endure a smoke-filled cabin even though the smokers were assigned to the rear seats, I was relieved to hear the engines change pitch and we prepared to make our descent towards Odessa.

The Black Sea City of Odessa, home to Gennadi and many other Soviet crew with whom I had worked, was fairly familiar to me. We had docked there many times in the past, mainly to allow a change of crew; almost all of them had families and children and they looked forward to spending a few weeks together, before re-joining the same vessel or possibly a different one. It was also an opportunity to offload the many items they had purchased during the cruises, which could be anything from electrical equipment to toiletries and the most popular piece of clothing—jeans.

I recalled the tours I had made with the passengers on board ship, which was the only way I could go ashore without a visa. The city was rather dull, in the usual communist way, apart from the Opera House and the striking Potemkin Steps and other architectural buildings constructed in the last century or two.

The queues outside the small shops always fascinated but saddened me, and I wondered what they were actually queuing for and if they finally received it. I never knew, as we were not allowed to stop near the local shops or cafes, apart from our final point of interest, the *Beriozka* shop—a shop solely for tourists and foreign currency. It was here we could buy Russian champagne, Stolichnaya vodka, handmade shawls, beautiful handcrafted wooden stacking dolls (*matriochki*), trinket boxes and a careful selection of Russian literature.

After landing and passing through customs and immigration, where my visa and passport were scrutinised thoroughly, I was greeted by a smiling face that was all too familiar—Dermot. How reassuring it was to see him again and as he kissed my cheek and grabbed my bag, we caught a taxi to the small Intourist hotel I had booked in the centre of the city.

'How was Moscow, Lou?' he asked.

'Bitterly cold, Dermot, but Stefan entertained me brilliantly,' I replied cheerfully. He raised his eyebrows questionably, but I was quick to add, 'Stefan is the perfect gentlemen and respects the fact that I am in love with Gennadi. I believe he has a family somewhere, but we didn't discuss his personal affairs.'

'No need to explain, darling, I was only teasing. I know Gennadi is the light of your life,' said Dermot, grinning.

Checking in and dumping my bag in the room, I was excited to see Katya again, so without wasting any more time, we jumped into another taxi and headed for the flat Dermot shared with her and her *babushka*. There was no snow here and it wasn't quite so cold, but the air was damp and there was a flurry of sleet on the windscreen.

Arriving in a broad street of terraced houses we stopped and as Dermot opened the door to a modest ground floor flat, I walked into a dark room and was immediately engulfed in a warm embrace by Katya.

'I am so excited to see you again, Louisa,' said the attractive girl I remembered on board ship. Slim and delicate with long, waist-length, light brown hair, large green eyes and a pretty smile. She was looking more relaxed now, as Dermot put his arms around both of us and gave us a hug.

'And I am so happy to be here for your wedding, Katya,' I replied. 'I feel we have all waited so long for this to actually happen. I can't quite believe the day has finally arrived. How lucky you both are and what an exciting future is waiting for you.'

'Thank you, Louisa. But I know you have Gennadi on your mind and I will do my best to help you find him.'

At that moment, an older woman, in a colourful headscarf and worn slippers, entered the room bringing a tray of drinks and *zakuski*. She smiled, displaying gold teeth as she proceeded to set the tray of Russian delicacies on the table. Many Russians I knew, including Gennadi, would have their teeth filled or capped with gold. This precious metal was almost immune to corrosion and, although strange to Western eyes, seemed to be the preferred filling used by Soviet contemporary dentists.

'My dear *babushka*. Louisa, I would like to introduce you,' said Katya.

'*Zdrastvuytie, kak dela*?' I said confidently.

'*Zdrastvuytie, dorogaya. Dobro pozhalovat,*' replied the old lady kindly, giving me a hug.

I remember Dermot had told me a while ago that Katya's parents lived in Siberia. This revelation had shocked me at the time, and it wasn't until he told me that they had relocated to that part of the country by choice that I recovered myself and tentatively asked him why. To foreigners Siberia was a vast area of unpopulated land, cut off from civilisation with long, harsh winters and very little chance of leaving once you were there. I thought mainly political prisoners had been sent there to labour camps for eternal exile—a cruel and incomprehensible prospect.

According to Katya, this current idea was attributed to Stalin, who expanded on the tsars' original plan of sending undesirables to live in this remote region (some even continuing to receive pensions under the tsar). But Stalin was more ruthless and exiled about 10 million people to Siberia, for forced labour in the mines and forests.

However, since then, in the 1950s, Khrushchev wanted to attract settlers in the mines, hydro-electric factories and on collective farms, to produce more corn and grain, to help supply the huge demand needed to feed a hungry nation. The wages were high and there were special bonuses to be awarded, so Katya's parents decided to take the plunge. They seemed settled there and Katya travelled to see them each summer if she could. Nevertheless, there are of course many political prisoners, who are still regularly sent there against their will, and it was this stark fact that currently occupied my busy mind, more than anything else.

Now, we gathered around the table and helped ourselves to a variety of simple but tasty Russian *zakuski,* and toasted each other with Russian *shampanskoye* and vodka. How pleasant it was to be among friends and share their happiness and how I hoped with all my heart, that we would be able to find Gennadi and fulfil the longing I had to be with him again.

I spent the rest of the day chatting with Dermot and helping Katya and her *babushka* prepare the food for a few friends, who would gather here after the wedding ceremony for a small celebration. Then as afternoon turned to evening, I realised how exhausted I was feeling—mainly due to the constant anguish of possibly never finding Gennadi rather than the journey involved in getting here.

Back in my hotel room, sipping some tea I had ordered from reception, I thought of the possibilities tomorrow might bring. We had one full day before the wedding, which had been arranged for the day after tomorrow, and I was reluctant to monopolise Katya. She had assured me that all was ready for the simple registry office procedure, but even so, I felt it was selfish to expect her to trail around Odessa, without much information other than Gennadi's full name. She didn't seem to know any of his friends either, as they had been on board the *Ukraina* at different times.

I never did receive Gennadi's home address, for some reason. The family he was supposed to have probably did exist and my pursuit of him could, quite likely, cause scandal and pain. I conveyed these thoughts to Katya but she, ever the romantic, insisted that she would search the city's phone book and ask her friends if they knew of Gennadi's whereabouts. I had come too far to stop looking now.

My prayers that night were fervent, and I honestly don't remember, up until then, of ever asking for anything with such earnest passion as I did that night in Odessa—to find Gennadi.

Worn out, physically and mentally, I managed to make myself as comfortable as possible in the small and somewhat hard, single bed pressed up against the wall, and eventually drifted off to sleep.

20

The Search

True to her word, Katya had found two G. Potenkos in the local phone book and when I met her outside the hotel first thing the next morning, my mixed emotions were of intense excitement tinged with nervous apprehension. The air was cold and the pedestrians on the street were wrapped up against the chilly wind. I was glad of my coat and solid, weatherproof boots but I still hadn't managed to find a hat that Stefan had so sensibly recommended. Katya was wearing a red wool one and as Dermot never wore headgear, maybe she thought we foreigners didn't like them.

'Ready, Louisa? We will take the tram to this first address. It's not far,' she said with her confident smile.

We crossed the street and almost at once, the tram arrived. We boarded it quickly before being whisked off to another part of the city. It was packed full of people and Katya and I ended up sitting next to other commuters, who gave me the usual inquisitive glance before staring out of the grubby window again. The old buildings gradually got shabbier and more rundown, when Katya signalled to me to get ready to leave the tram at the next stop.

Looking around at the grey, gloominess of the tall flats and the street we had to traverse in order to access them, I was having serious doubts about finding Gennadi. Surely, he couldn't live in an area like this after the bright, clean crew quarters on board ship? It must have been raining recently, as there were dirty-looking puddles leading up to some of the doorways and someone had placed planks over the grimy water. Katya and I carefully crossed over one of them, balancing like tightrope walkers, to avoid slipping and spoiling our nice clean boots.

Few people were around as it was a working day; getting her bearings, Katya followed the apartment numbers till she stopped and led me towards a door that was standing ajar. This, Katya said, was the first address she had found and as we ascended the stairs, my eyes were drawn to the graffiti on the walls (in Cyrillic, of course, and making no sense to me at all), amidst the damp patches and peeling paintwork. How awful to live here and being so cold at this time of year, the occupants would have a hard job keeping warm. Fuel was not cheap and they wouldn't have the luxury of central heating. My heart sank as I imagined my Gennadi—and maybe his family—calling this home.

Finally, reaching our destination on the third floor, where the distinct smell of *Shchi* (cabbage soup) was emanating, Katya looked at me expectantly and gave the door a hard knock. My heart pounded in my chest as we stood looking towards the door, then at each other, wondering if our presence had been noticed. A minute or two passed and we heard the sound of shuffling feet, then the door opened a few centimetres and a wrinkled face appeared, wearing a headscarf. Another *babushka* left at home to prepare the meal, whilst the younger members of the family were hard at work somewhere in the city. Katya spoke a few words and the old woman shook her head. I heard the name Grisha mentioned. So, there was a Grisha Potenko living here but not a Gennadi.

As the door closed, a heavy sigh escaped me and I felt overwhelmingly disappointed but at the same time slightly relieved that Gennadi didn't have to live in such a place as this.

'Don't worry, Louisa, *dorogaya*,' said Katya, my despondency clearly visible. 'We have another address to investigate.'

'Yes, Katya, thank you. I really appreciate you doing this, especially as tomorrow is such an important day for you and Dermot.'

'Yes, Lou, but you have only two more days left in Odessa, and we must find Gennadi. '

Descending the stairway and completing the obstacle course over the planks, Katya tried to hail a taxi. Finally, a little box-like car slowed down and stopped beside us, but it didn't appear to have a taxi sign displayed. I asked her why.

'This is a private car, Louisa, not a proper taxi. Some people risk giving illegal lifts for cash. We have a big black market here.'

I nodded, as she proceeded to tell the driver our required address.

After a while, we passed the Potemkin Steps—all 192 of which I had climbed in the past—and presently stopped in a tree-lined avenue with big grand-looking, though dilapidated, houses. This was more civilised, I thought, and as I gazed at the faded, yellow painted facades of ornate, huge-windowed buildings, I could imagine how they used to look in the time of the tsars. Well-dressed people exiting their carriages whilst a servant, beautifully attired, waited to open the immense front door.

Katya paid our driver with the roubles I had insisted she should take and led the way towards the next address she had written down.

'The houses here have been converted into many flats during the early Soviet times,' she said, as I followed her towards a house with a wall surrounding it and a gap where the gate used to be. 'They may have families of eight or ten people living in one small one. Come, let's see if someone is at home.'

The knots in my stomach began to tighten as we approached the main door, where I saw an elderly man digging in a scrap of a garden. I wondered what he was growing in this cold, damp climate—maybe beetroot, cabbage or potatoes—essential nutritious consumables most Russians couldn't live without. He looked up as we drew closer. Wearing a flat cap and clothing that had seen better days, he stopped his work and leant on his spade, as Katya introduced herself and began to explain why we were here.

He looked at me quizzically and Katya said in Russian, 'We are looking for Gennadi Potenko, a good friend of ours. Does he live here?'

The old man smiled when he heard the name, revealing a few remaining teeth, and my hopes rose as I eagerly strained to hear what he had to say.

'I am Pavel Potenko and my son is Georg. Are you sure you are looking for this Gennadi and not my son?'

I felt my shoulders sink and my eyes grow moist, as yet again a feeling of dejection swept over me. The old man noticed my disappointment with curiosity, peering at me from under his frayed cap, as we took our leave and wished him a good day. Walking back down the short, untidy driveway, I glanced back and saw him resume his digging, shaking his head and muttering something quietly to himself.

'I am so sorry, Louisa,' said Katya, looking unusually serious. 'You must not give up hope. I will continue asking around. Meanwhile,' she added cheerfully, 'let's go home and have lunch. *Babushka* will be waiting.'

21

Time Is Short

I resigned myself to the fact that we weren't going to find Gennadi that easily, if indeed at all. Odessa was a large city and he may live somewhere in the suburbs. I knew I must spend the rest of my short stay here exploring every possible path and leaving no stone unturned, in order to rule out any regrets I might have in the future.

Arriving back at Katya's flat, I realised that I was in fact very hungry. We had left soon after breakfast, which, for me, had been tea and two slices of black Russian bread with honey. So, we were both happy to find a table full of delicious, homemade Russian food that Katya's *babushka* had kindly prepared for us—borshch soup, pickled fish, pickled vegetables and black bread.

We had just begun to fill our bowls with soup and enjoy the warmth of the small gas fire underneath the mantelpiece, taking the place of an old coal one situated behind, when Dermot arrived, looking pleased with himself. This bolstered my confidence, and we all ate hungrily whilst exchanging news of our investigations.

'I managed to find some of Gennadi's old crewmates down at the docks,' he said cheerfully, as he stirred some sour cream into his bowl of borshch. 'They gave me directions where they thought he might live with his parents and sister. Only trouble is, they could have moved recently as there was talk of demolishing that area and building new blocks of flats. But we can go down there tomorrow, after the wedding,' he added, looking at me reassuringly.

'Yes Dermot, it's certainly worth a try,' I replied, trying to sound positive, though I felt we were clutching at straws.

The meal over, we sat and chatted for a while as we finished our cups of tea and *babushka* treated us to some *bliny* with sour cream, which she had made earlier—meltingly delicious. Russian Slavic history tells us that the pagan people worshipped the sun and they honoured their god at the spring solstice by cooking and eating his image—a thin golden batter cake fried in golden butter. To this day the Russians eat scores of *bliny*, particularly at *Maslenitsa*, or Butter Festival, that precedes the forty days of Lent. Unlike our simple pancakes, *bliny* are made of buckwheat flour and yeast and take several hours to prepare, letting the dough rest after each beating.

Feeling a sense of restlessness and a desire not to intrude further on the family today, I helped clear the table and said, 'It's getting late and there must be things you both want to do, so I'll leave you to it and meet you tomorrow morning. What time shall I be ready?'

'Let's meet here at ten and have some pre-wedding *shampanskoye*, Lou, just to calm the nerves before the big event.' He glanced quickly at Katya, who raised her eyebrows as he slid his arm around her, smiling tenderly. After such a long time waiting for this special occasion, neither of them could really believe the day was almost here.

'Yes, lovely,' I said and made my way out onto the quiet street to hail a taxi.

Not only did I want Katya and Dermot to have some private time, but I knew it was forbidden for foreigners to spend the night in a Russian home. There could be prying eyes watching the movements of people like Dermot and myself, and I certainly didn't want to be responsible for any awkward repercussions on my part. Dermot was practically married and accounted for, but I was not.

Securing a taxi surprisingly quickly, I did not return to my hotel immediately as I had an important mission to accomplish first. I had not brought a wedding present for Dermot and Katya from England, as I feared it might cause trouble going through customs at the airport. So, I asked the taxi driver to take me to the *Beriozka* shop in town, where I hoped to find something that might please the newlyweds. This shop was only for foreigners (or Russians who had obtained foreign currency), and they stocked a wide range of quality Russian goods. I had brought some dollars with me which I intended to spend there. This was, without doubt, the most sought-after method of payment.

The shop was fairly busy with mostly tour groups of Europeans, carefully choosing the items they wanted to take home as gifts or mementos. I passed the food section, containing caviar, Russian alcohol and various cured meats, followed by the literary corner, encompassing a wide range of Russian literature from past to present—all in Russian. Then a beautiful array of Russian folkloric, handmade goods lay temptingly on glass shelves lit with very bright lights. This enhanced the colourful, lacquered jewellery boxes, decorative wooden bowls with spoons and *matryoshki* and made them even more vibrant and attractive.

There was jewellery too; wonderful necklaces, bracelets and rings of amber from the north of Soviet Russia, arranged with care and glowing with a hue of warm, honey translucency. The Slavs had always loved this petrified tree resin and believed it was the tears of people, shed over the tombs of fallen heroes. They wore it close to their bodies to preserve good health.

But none of these gifts seemed fitting for my two friends' special wedding present, until my eyes were drawn to several large objects nearby, polished till they shone with their own reflected light and a symbol of Russia past and present—a row of silver *samovars*—a traditional Russian tea urn. This was what I had been searching for. Something they could use regularly at home, as well as being an attractive ornamental feature. I had noticed the absence of one in Katya's flat and was quite sure they would like it and chose a middle of the range *samovar*, which was just within my budget.

Since it was impractical for me to carry back to the hotel, I kindly asked the sales lady if she could arrange delivery to the address I gave her, sometime tomorrow afternoon. I carefully put the receipt in my bag, knowing that the customs officer at the airport would ask to see it before I left Odessa. All foreign currency had to be itemised before entry into the Soviet Union and accounted for on leaving—a system I found tedious but obligatory. I certainly did not want to get into further difficulties with Soviet officials.

Pleased with my purchase and feeling a genuine sense of accomplishment, I left the store and walked back the short distance through the cold and dimly lit streets to my small hotel, to spend another night wondering sadly if attending the wedding would be my only achievement on this trip to Odessa.

Shortly before I was due to arrive at my lodgings, I passed by a high wall that had fallen into disrepair. As I glanced towards the crumbling stones, I glimpsed an image that I was not expecting to see—the outline of a distinctive church cupola, rising amidst the extensively overgrown surroundings. I stopped abruptly and peering between the tumble of stones, I could just make out the wall of the church and two more smaller domes beneath the main one. My curiosity was instantly aroused, as it was regarding any historical building harking back to a more colourful Russian era, and I decided to make my way around the wall until I found an entrance. I was eager to explore the church in greater depth before the opportunity was lost and darkness descended once more.

I knew religion was still not within the doctrines of communism, but many Russians still held the faith and prayed at home or in one of the churches that was permitted to operate. I had never seen a working church in the Soviet Union, only ones that had been spared closure and turned into museums.

Turning a corner, I was rewarded by the appearance of two rusted metal gates, loosely linked together with a large rusty chain. It had been some time since the gates had been in use, judging by the sorry state of their condition, and I just stood there looking over them at the beautiful sight beyond. The church was small but intact, and the once glorious onion domes, each one topped with a Russian gold cross, still showed some fragments of gold leaf but no longer gleamed brightly against the pale grey sky.

The narrow, arched windows below had been crudely boarded up with strips of uneven wood and most of the glass in between was broken and jagged. An immense sense of sadness, tinged with anger, overcame me and I came to an instant decision. Looking closely at the gate again and glancing around at the few pedestrians, hurrying along towards their destinations, I swiftly bent down and squeezed between the gap made by the sagging chain and suddenly found myself inside the churchyard. Although the bushes and wild flowers had long ago taken over the spacious grounds, I noticed the remnants of a barely detectable path. So hastening through the tangle of weeds and greenery, I endeavoured to make my way towards the church's main entrance.

Looking up, the great stone walls, once strong and beautifully painted, loomed high above me but now they were peeling and patches of plaster had fallen away in places. My boots got caught in some thick creeping vine and I very nearly tripped and fell, just managing to keep my balance, and was very glad to see that I had finally reached the end of the track. The grand entrance stood directly in front of me and I was not surprised to see that the two wooden double doors had also been chained together, and were inevitably showing the ravages of time. They had faded and decayed in parts but on closer inspection, I could just make out intricate, faint carvings round the outer edge of each door and the remains of several metal studs. Perhaps for fifty years or more, they had stood undisturbed, barring access to the faithful, until this building was ultimately forgotten and just part of the landscape of another era.

It was Stalin who had closed the churches and monasteries, I remembered reading from my Russian history books, and arrested priests or sent them into exile. The Orthodox church had become too powerful during the tsars' rule and in order to sever the ties of the past, Stalin could not sanction the practice of religion. The tsars had ruled 'in the name of God,' dazzling the faithful with displays of shining gold icons, jewelled ornaments, perfumed candles and colourful frescoes adorning the walls and ceilings of the 'Palaces of God.' The congregation would not sit in pews but stand and listen to the priest's praying and chanting, sometimes for hours on end, and they would invariably come and go as they pleased, for they were in God's house.

Stalin's power, however, was manifested in impressive military parades, police enforcements and the pursuit of an atheist ideology, endeavouring ultimate control of the people. He feared any link with the church could be dangerous for himself and for the future of communism.

But with the coming of war, he desperately needed more support against the Germans and, in 1941, he relaxed his anti-religious ideals and ceased the anti-religious propaganda. He made peace with the Patriarch and other religious leaders in Russia, and services were again permitted and churches consequently crowded. This proved a solace to the people during these troubled years even though the priests, in memory of their unwavering support for the tsar, ironically encouraged the people to obey their current atheist leader and defend their country.

I was still standing facing the old doors when, on impulse, I reached out and touched the tarnished, metal doorknob. It was stiff and would not turn as I expected. How I would love to pass through this doorway and light a candle for Gennadi, see it flicker against the walls and ceilings till it burned down to the sand, and imagine that I was not the only visitor in God's house that day. I closed my eyes and I could almost hear the chanting, feel the warm bodies standing close to mine and smell the fragrant incense enveloping me in a comforting warm embrace. I crossed myself in the Western style, as I had been taught, and prayed that Gennadi was safe and all would be well.

A loud, echoing crash suddenly came from within the church, making my whole body jump and set my heart pounding like a galloping horse out of control. I looked around me; the sky was dark and all I could see was the faint outline of the wall around the church grounds. How long had I been standing here? How could I have been so foolish? I must leave immediately but how was I to find the way out? And what on earth was that noise I just heard? A few moments of panic hit me with unexpected force and my whole body trembled. I desperately scanned my surroundings for the path I had followed and the gate at the end of it. At any moment, I was expecting someone to appear and reprimand me, or at worst, arrest me for trespassing.

Talking quietly to myself and urging calm at all costs, I took a deep breath and immediately took control of the situation. I would head towards the nearest part of the wall, which was now only barely visible, and follow it around till I eventually found the chained metal gates. This seemed like a sensible plan and putting it into immediate action, I started to pick my way through the dense foliage, my eyes focused on the wall ahead, my ears alert for any possible danger and my heart still thumping in my chest. What I would have done if I had heard footsteps or voices anywhere near me, I do not know, but I soon realised that my eyes were registering clearer images and I arrived at the wall sooner than I expected.

Touching the cold stones, I looked up and saw the clouds thinning, allowing some opaque moonlight to shine down and guide my footsteps along the perimeter. Very soon, the familiar gates were within sight. My pulse had steadied now and holding onto the top bar of one gate, I crouched down, pushing hard as I forced my body through the gap and back onto the deserted road outside.

Hurrying to join the main thoroughfare again, I cast one more look behind me and hesitated momentarily, as I saw the shape of a sleek cat jump up onto the wall by the gate and sit there, silhouetted against the sky. For a few seconds, it regarded me with mild interest before leaping down and vanishing into the gloom in the opposite direction. I smiled to myself, for I now knew the probable source of the noise in the church that had startled me and was glad that the explanation had revealed itself.

It was a short walk along the quiet street before I saw the welcome lights of my little hotel, and I was immensely relieved to be back at last. It was very cold and the clouds had gathered again, so I wasn't even able to make out the time on my watch, but I believed it was past dinner time and the kitchen would, no doubt, be closed.

I had guessed correctly and pushing open the front door and into the warmth of the foyer, the receptionist greeted me with a stiff smile, as he handed me my key and informed me that dinner had finished half an hour ago. I returned his smile and asked only if I may take a hot drink up to my room.

Lying on my narrow bed in my cupboard-like grey, Intourist room, I went over the day's events as I drank my tea and ate a Mars bar I had brought with me from England. It was all much more difficult than I had ever imagined. Why, oh why, had Gennadi not left me his address? There could only be one reason. How I wish I knew one way or the other. It would certainly help me determine the future.

As I lay there, I thought of Gennadi going about his work somewhere in Odessa and prayed again that I would find him before I left the Soviet Union. I only had one more full day here before my visa expired and my return flight took me back to England; possibly my last chance of ever discovering the truth about him.

I slept fitfully that night and somewhere in my dreams, I imagined being surrounded by shining, golden icons and aromatic incense, and I was standing beside Gennadi in a Russian church, lighting a candle and sharing the magic of an Orthodox service. He was smiling and looking happier than I had ever seen him, before the image quickly faded and I fell into a deeper, dreamless but more restful sleep.

22

A Day of Celebration

Waking early, I went down to reception and the small area that was occupied with a couple of tables set for breakfast. I ordered tea and black bread with marmalade. There was no milk as usual—it was always in short supply—but the tea was refreshing, and I was used to drinking it now without the addition of milk. Maybe I would continue with this Russian custom when I arrived back home again.

There were no other guests around and my mind returned to the plans for today, desperately trying to come up with more ideas to locate Gennadi. Should I go to the Black Sea shipping offices and ask for his contact details? No, that would only cause trouble and probably result in me being warned to discontinue my search altogether. I would have to be content with Dermot's idea and hope we could find someone at this other address who knew Gennadi, his sister or their parents.

Donning my warm, fur coat and boots, together with my cosy gloves, I checked my camera and flashgun and made my way over to join Katya and Dermot for a celebratory drink. As I had plenty of time, I decided to walk instead of taking the usual taxi. It was a bright day, though not sunny, and I felt half an hour or so at a brisk pace would do me good and I could sample the life of Odessa, mingling with the pedestrians going about their business. I knew my presence would be remarked upon but I sensed no danger amongst the Soviet people, and I secretly wished that maybe someone from the ship might recognise me and report back to Gennadi—a fanciful idea, but one that fostered a hint of optimism and kept my spirits buoyant. The streets were busy as usual with women forming long queues outside various food shops, looking cold and weary, and other folk filling the antique-looking buses and trams far beyond their intended capacity.

As I approached the street where the taxi usually turned off, I saw a barrier with arrows that directed the public to continue further down the main road. The reason for this was roadworks going on and as I passed by, there were women at work alongside the men, operating machinery that looked heavy and cumbersome. The fact that they were wearing brightly coloured headscarves made them stand out from their male colleagues and my eyes rested on them a little longer. I was still not used to seeing women doing jobs here, which in the Western world were performed only by men. It was, however, a common sight in the Soviet Union, where women were employed in many sectors of society, enabling them to readily contribute to the family income and relieve the labour shortage.

I carried on down the road till more signs pointed to the next turning and I knew Katya's house was nearby. I felt a cold wind sweep across my face and ruffle my hair and I drew the collar of my fur coat closer, dodging the potholes and puddles in the street. Maybe it would snow after all, making the hardship of a Soviet winter even more challenging.

'You both look wonderful!' I exclaimed, as the radiant couple stood before me in the little sitting room, champagne glasses in hand and the light shining from the small window onto their happy faces. Katya wore a below-the-knee, slinky, red dress and her brown hair was tied with red carnations at the nape of her neck, letting it flow silkily down her back. Dermot was his usual relaxed self in a blazer with collar and tie; his copper hair neatly brushed, his beard trimmed and his blue eyes sparkling. He had also, much to my surprise, exchanged his familiar moccasins for a smart pair of pristine, shiny leather shoes.

My camera was clicking like mad, as I strove to capture their joyful expressions whilst they posed and laughed unselfconsciously, a look of mild disbelief on their faces that this day had arrived at last. Glancing at Katya's *babushka*, I saw she was beaming with undisguised pleasure, and I knew she had also longed for this day when her dearest granddaughter would fulfil her dreams. She must have realised that Katya would probably leave her home in Odessa eventually, if permitted. But Katya would most definitely return regularly if she could, to see her dear *babushka* and parents who only wanted the very best for their precious girl's future.

It all seemed so perfect and I was drawn into this circle of happiness, experiencing a profound sense of pleasure at being able to witness this special day.

Without any kind of warning, there was a sudden, loud rap at the door. We all looked towards the source of the noise and a moment of silence followed, surprise evident on our faces, as we each tried to interpret the meaning of this unexpected interruption. What happened next remains clearly etched in my mind to this day and the euphoric atmosphere of a few seconds ago was replaced with one of intense foreboding. Standing immobile as if transfixed in time, with all my senses heightened and my fears rising, the silence continued, save for the ticking of the old clock on the mantelpiece as it counted the seconds leading up to the events that were shortly to follow.

Putting down her glass with a look of curiosity on her pretty, smiling face, Katya walked towards the door. My pulse rate increased as I desperately considered who it might be. Had I been careless and irresponsible in my quest to find Gennadi? Had the authorities decided to curtail my visit or, worse, take retribution on my dear friends? Please God, not on their wedding day! Not after all this!

My body was becoming uncomfortably tense, my breathing rapid, as Katya reached for the handle and I had a sudden vision of the chief purser on the *Ukraina*, leering at me and gloating over my miserable predicament. Each second dragged slowly into the next and my heartbeat threatened to deafen me, as the door opened slightly, still shielding the visitor from view.

An unexpected frisson of excitement swept through me as the stranger spoke quietly in Russian and Katya replied, gasping and stepping falteringly backwards, her eyes huge, as the door swung fully open. Dermot rushed to her side, and all our eyes were now drawn towards the figure in the doorway.

A man's shadowy silhouette, clad in a knee-length coat, his back to the light, obscuring his features, was now stepping over the threshold and entering the room, allowing light from the little window to fall onto his face and reveal his identity at last.

The frenzy of the moment escalated, and a cry of intense pleasure escaped my lips, as my eyes took in the familiar sight of the man I loved. 'Gennadi!' I cried breathlessly, looking into his dark, brown eyes and handsome face, shining with happiness. As if in a dream, I moved quickly towards his outstretched arms and fell into his embrace. But this was no dream for I felt his arms tighten possessively around my body and cover my face with his loving kisses.

'Louisa, *dorogaya*,' he whispered tenderly, as I returned his kisses and clung fiercely to his waist lest he vanish as quickly as he had appeared. There were cries of 'bravo' from my friends, followed by a flurry of questions and everyone talking at once. No one could quite believe what we were witnessing. I was overwhelmed with relief and happiness. My frantic search was over, and *I* was the one to be found. I felt intoxicated with happiness and my spirits soared with unconcealed delight.

There was much talk and laughter by us all and toast after toast, until Dermot looked at the clock and suggested we leave for the registry office before it was too late or they'd have to make another appointment for the wedding—perhaps in a year or so!

23

Time to Explain

Hurrying to the registry office located on the other side of town, the four of us crammed into a little taxi and talking constantly in a mixture of Russian and English, we proceeded to unravel the mystery of Gennadi's sudden and dramatic appearance. He held my hand tightly as he began to explain, hardly taking his eyes off me for a moment.

By amazing coincidence, he just happened to be walking down the street where Katya lived—not knowing Katya at all well, let alone where she resided. He had some time off work and was on his way to see a friend, when he caught sight of a woman in a large fur coat, bushy dark hair and an attitude that he was sure he recognised. Quickening his step, so as not to lose her amongst the other pedestrians, he watched as she crossed the road and was ushered into a small flat.

He broke off laughing and said he thought he might have imagined seeing the woman, as Louisa had dominated his thoughts for weeks and he wasn't quite sure of anything anymore. I nodded and squeezed his hand as he continued, 'My heart was telling me to go to the flat and knock on the door, and although I still wasn't sure it was you, Louisa, nothing was going to stop me from doing it.' He held me close and looked at me so lovingly, I realised how lucky I was and said a quiet prayer of thanks that destiny had so far favoured us.

The taxi slowed down and Katya exclaimed excitedly, her eyes shining, 'We're here. Let's go!'

We all bundled out onto the pavement and I saw the grey steps leading up to the doors of the registry office; as Katya and Dermot began to climb them, Gennadi looked at me and I smiled, acknowledging his thoughts as they mirrored mine, wishing with all my heart that this could be our special day too.

The simple ceremony, in a little room on the second floor, was over very quickly. Dermot had learnt his words in Russian and executed them perfectly and Katya looked amazingly calm and very beautiful as she too made her vows. I tried hard to follow along but was distracted by Gennadi, whose eyes were nearly always turned towards me in deep adoration.

Soon, we all headed downstairs again and stopped halfway beside a huge mirror to take some memorable photographs of the newlyweds. Then out onto the street, where Katya asked the taxi driver to take a shot of all four of us as we laughed and hugged each other on the steps, not quite believing what had just taken place.

Gennadi and I waved to the taxi as it carried the dazed couple away, back to their home as man and wife, to continue a quiet celebration with her *babushka* and a few close friends and begin a new, though undetermined, future together.

Putting his arm around me, Gennadi and I headed off down the street in the direction of the city centre. So much to say and do and not enough time. We passed a busy flower market and he led me to a stall where there was an amazing selection of roses, all in a variety of colours. The Russians must love roses more than any other flower, as they always featured most predominantly in the beautiful displays on board ship. At Gennadi's insistence, I chose a small bouquet of a bright yellow variety with a heavenly scent, and the fragrance surrounded us as we continued walking towards a small cafe. We sat together in a corner, as close as we dared, and proceeded to discuss all that had taken place since we parted and some of what had happened before.

Our tea arrived, with a plate of *pirozhki* and a bowl of individually wrapped chocolates. Feeling quite hungry after all the morning's excitement, I readily helped myself to one of the tasty little meat pastries as Gennadi began his story.

Speaking slowly and gravely, Gennadi's first words confirmed my deepest dread, that he was indeed married; but he was quick to add that he and his wife had lived separately for some time. He had a daughter too, an eight-year-old, whom he saw as often as he was physically able, when not at sea. These revelations, so truthfully admitted, should not have shocked me as they did and it took me a few minutes to digest all he was saying, until I was compelled to ask why he had not told me before.

'I was afraid you would not want to continue our relationship and think I only wanted an affair,' he said nervously, clearly still not certain of my reaction to this latest disclosure.

After a moment or two, I looked up into his impassioned eyes and he continued, 'The last time we met with Vladimir as interpreter, I was longing to tell you the truth but apart from being forbidden to do so, as I said in my letter, there was a tape recorder in the room and they recorded everything we said,' he acknowledged sadly.

I had heard about this common procedure in the Soviet world, but was surprised that the authorities deemed our relationship important enough to bother to use this system, on this occasion. It seemed that any encounter between a Russian citizen and a foreigner was worth a certain amount of scrutiny, and the fact that I was sitting opposite Gennadi at this very moment was indeed miraculous.

I glanced around nervously at the other customers in the room, wondering if we had actually been followed that very day and our conversation, though muted, was consequently being committed to tape. But after a brief, inquisitive glance in our direction when we entered, the few other occupants appeared to be in deep conversation with their respective partners or just enjoying the time to relax within a busy Soviet regime.

Gennadi, studying my expression, guessed what was going through my mind and said quietly, 'It's all right, *dorogaya*, we are alone here. No one else knows. It's just you and me at last. I have longed for this day ever since you left the ship and I swore that I would try to find you again.'

'Oh, Gennadi,' I began. But before I could say more, he was leaning forward and kissing me very firmly on my lips, dispelling any immediate thoughts of possible danger. He was just about to withdraw when I held him there, savouring the precious moments I had so often dreamt about.

Releasing him at last, I looked guiltily around the cafe and noticed that the other clients in this typically Soviet, starkly decorated little place, seemed indifferent to our presence. But the young waitress who had served us, quickly looked away, smiling as she busied herself with the clatter of cups and saucers behind the counter.

'Gennadi, what of our future?' I asked tentatively. 'Is there any hope of us being together?'

I thought of his wife and child and how complicated it all seemed to be. Was it fair to think about pursuing a relationship when language, distance and politics stood in our way?

He looked suddenly very serious and taking both my hands in his, said solemnly, 'Louisa, *dorogaya*. I love you more than anyone in this world and if it is possible to spend the rest of my life with you, I will do almost anything to achieve it.' His expression mirrored the impassioned sincerity of his words, and I was filled with such a profound and reciprocating love for this man, that for a moment, I struggled to voice my next words.

'But your family? Your daughter? Your parents? How will they react to this news? Would they ever accept me, a foreigner from the West, who has stolen their father and son from them and has, perhaps, created problems for them in the future?'

Gennadi, his voice steady and his face as reassuring as ever, replied with complete ease, 'I have told my parents and my sister, Lyudmila, all about you already. I had to. I could not keep this secret for long. They deserved to know the truth about us and I knew they would understand. We are a close family and stand by each other in times of trouble.'

I was heartened to hear this as he continued, 'My parents are happy for the love I feel for you but they foresee difficulties and obstacles in our path. My sister, however, longs to meet you one day and is very optimistic and excited about our future together. Do not worry, *dorogaya*, their life

165

will not change because of us. I will apply for an official divorce and it will be accepted very quickly, as my wife and I have been separated for so long. Then I will be free to marry you, if that is what you truly wish.'

His face was full of hope and confidence, and he made it all sound so simple as though everything would fall into place, and I was quickly swept along on this tide of near certainty.

'That is something I have been dreaming of, my love,' I said with sincere passion. 'I will arrange my next visit to Odessa as soon as possible, as long as the authorities are willing to grant me a visa again. I shall have to come up with a very good reason for coming back so quickly.'

'Yes, *lyubimaya*. I will be waiting for you.'

We hugged each other tightly and finishing our tea and chocolates, talked of other things. The electrical work he was now doing in Odessa in several new hotels, and the crew members we both knew and how happy they would be to see me again when I returned.

Then, taking my hand firmly in his, he said brightly, 'Come, Louisa. I want to show you the best shops in Odessa.'

24

Evening in Odessa

It was getting quite dark by the time we left the little cafe and stepped out onto the cold grey, streets. I held my bouquet of roses carefully cradled in one arm, whilst Gennadi guided me towards a brighter, busier part of the city, where other residents hurried to finish their shopping, before returning home to enjoy their evening meal and attempt to keep warm.

A large ornate building loomed up ahead and as we drew closer, I immediately identified its circular form and beautiful Italian Baroque style facade—the Odessa Opera House. I had been here many times in the past, accompanying the ship's passengers to see several ballet performances, the most popular being *Giselle*. The large entrance doors were firmly closed but a light shone in a glass cabinet nearby, displaying various faded colour photographs of the dancers performing one of their famous ballets.

'Look Gennadi,' I exclaimed, 'they are still dancing *Giselle*. I must have seen it two or three times. Such a sad story and how beautiful the ballerinas were in their long white dresses.'

The ballet is the pride of all Russians, a delight of the tsarist era and continuing into the Soviet one. Hundreds of children apply for the Bolshoi every year but only thirty or forty are accepted, and the remainder end up joining smaller ballet companies in provincial capitals, such as here in Odessa, where they will probably spend the rest of their lives. The technical skills the Soviet dancers were capable of certainly increased year by year but they lacked inspiration and originality, therefore restricting the range of classical works performed.

Tickets for the ballet, however, would often be sold out weeks ahead and I recalled a story a passenger once told me, about an American diplomat's wife in Moscow, who wanted to give her Russian maid a Christmas gift. The American gave the maid a magazine, in which she could choose a new dress in the latest Parisian fashion but the maid, though grateful, replied, 'Thank you, but I would rather have a ticket to see the Bolshoi ballet please.'

Lost in my thoughts for a moment, I turned to Gennadi and saw that he was also looking at the photos with some interest. 'Did you ever see them perform, Gennadi?' I asked, half-expecting him to say he never had the time or opportunity.

He looked at me oddly, then smiled and said, 'Yes Louisa, many times. You see, my wife's sister is one of the dancers here. That's her there,' he said, pointing to a pretty dark-haired girl in the picture.

'Oh, how wonderful,' I replied, experiencing a strange mixture of emotions I could not quite describe.

'Look,' said Gennadi, glancing at his watch, 'it is 5 o'clock already and we need to see the shops and have dinner somewhere. Our time is short, *dorogaya*,' he added with a sad smile.

He was right. Only a few hours left of this blissful day, and tomorrow I would be flying away from him yet again. But this time it was different, I knew I would try to be back again very soon, with a definite path to follow and Gennadi by my side.

We looked at many shops in the city centre but to my Western eyes, they were a sad representation of luxury goods—chocolates, toiletries and clothes—quite dull and drab, with limited selections and very unimaginatively presented and displayed. I am sure Gennadi guessed what I might be thinking. He had seen what the West could offer, but he appeared determined that I should find some memento he could buy that I could take home to remind me of this extraordinary day.

As we strolled arm in arm from one department to the next, our boots resonating noisily on the old wooden floorboards, I became aware of the recorded music I could hear in the background of one large store. The sound was so crackly, it reminded me of an old record player that was in desperate need of a new needle. I pretended not to notice as we continued our search, and I mentally compared this shop to the *Beriozka* shops. These outlets were far more interesting and were filled with the colour and ambience of a Russia long ago, a country the foreign visitors preferred to see, rather than the present, sombre Soviet one. But here I was in Odessa with my dearest Gennadi and I was having difficulty finding that special something. Perhaps I would just settle for a new pair of gloves or another Russian shawl—I so wanted to please him.

It wasn't until we entered the fur shop, that I at last knew what I clearly needed and wanted. As I took in all the fur coats, hats, scarves and gloves, I had a vision of Stefan, in Moscow, gently scolding me for not wearing a cosy hat, in true Muscovite tradition. Observing my immediate enthusiasm when I walked towards a shelf full of beautiful fur hats, Gennadi looked delighted that I had finally found a gift I truly wanted. The stocky middle-aged shop assistant approached us, carrying a small mirror, which she propped on the shelf, and cordially invited me to try on any of the hats on display.

'How do I look, Gennadi?' I asked, feeling a little self-conscious as I posed in the mirror, admiring the silver-grey hat that almost matched the colour of my coat.

'*Ochen krasivah*, Louisa *lyubimaya*,' he replied with a broad smile. As he peered over my shoulder, my eyes instantly shifted from my own reflection to that of his, realising that this was the first time I had actually seen our faces side by side. We never did manage to have our photograph taken together on the ship, and besides, if we had, it would have been fatal if discovered by the wrong person. I lingered over this new visual experience for several long seconds, and came quickly to the conclusion that our colouring and features were really quite similar; dark eyes, dark hair, full lips and skin that turned a honey shade of brown in the sun.

A gentle hand touched my shoulder and Gennadi brought me back to the present. Turning around, I saw the shop assistant's expectant face, waiting for my decision.

'I think this hat is perfect—thank you, Gennadi,' I said with genuine enthusiasm.

'Now we must eat,' he said, looking relieved. As we left the shop, a cold wind hit us with such force, I clutched the

170

roses to my breast and felt Gennadi's strong arm around my waist, drawing me close in a protective embrace. There were fewer pedestrians around now, as the shops were closing and the time for the evening meal had begun. Most people would return home to eat, but a few who could afford it and visitors from other parts might dine out in Odessa's hotels and restaurants.

Hailing a small taxi, we drove down towards the harbour, and in a few minutes, we arrived beside a brightly lit, galleon-style, wooden sailing ship, moored to the quayside. The masts were strung with a myriad of white lights, and more soft lights shone from each porthole window. The wind had died down slightly but still the vessel creaked and swayed softly, pulling gently on the mooring ropes.

As I took in this amazing spectacle, quite surprising me amidst all the Soviet order, I asked why we were here. Gennadi proceeded to explain, 'This is a very popular restaurant, Louisa. I hope you will enjoy the food here. I felt it was right for us to finish our evening on a ship—as that was also where our life together first began.'

Hugging his arm and feeling again an indescribable mixture of joy and sadness, the only thing I wanted right now was to preserve this day for as long as possible. But the painful fact was that the clock kept on ticking, seemingly ever faster and the few hours we had left, were rapidly being swallowed up by an invisible force we could not control.

He led me carefully across the small wooden gangway and immediately turned left, ducking our heads under a doorway and descending a few stairs to the deck below, where the dining area was located. There were about seven or eight tables arranged in close proximity. Most were full, and one large group of diners in the centre were talking, laughing and toasting and appeared so engrossed in their meal and each other, that they never turned their heads when we entered.

A waiter, dressed in black trousers and a red, satin shirt greeted us courteously and led us to a table for two in a corner, which seemed a little darker and more discreet than the others. Leaving our coats on a spare chair, we settled on a bench covered in soft, decorative cushions and I watched Gennadi's animated face, in the mellow light of the table lamp, as he placed our order for dinner.

Our attention was then drawn to the party of men seated at the central table. They were all swarthy-skinned, dark-haired and dark-eyed, middle-aged men. Each had a very elaborate curly moustache and was speaking a language I had never heard before; totally unlike the familiar Russian I was used to. They were happily drinking small glasses of vodka and tucking into the many plates of *zakuski* that covered their table, when Gennadi explained, 'They are from Gruziya, Louisa, and I don't understand their language either!' he added, appearing amused as he studied my puzzled expression.

Gruziya, or Georgia, I learnt later, is situated on the southern slope of the Caucasus mountains, between the Black Sea and the Caspian Sea. They are a Christian race and only became part of the Russian Empire at the beginning of the 19th century. Gruziyans love to spend time with friends and family and, best of all, when sharing food and drink. Their land is wonderfully fertile, especially in the tropical coastal villages, and not only do they grow grapes, lemons, olives and almonds but the red and white local wine is very good too.

'A captain from Gruziya, on one of my previous ships, once told me that I could pass for a girl from his country,' I told Gennadi, as our waiter returned with *zakuski*, wine and a vase for my thirsty roses.

'Yes, *dorogaya*, that is true, you have the dark looks, but you would also have to master the language which has its own unique and beautiful written script, quite unlike our Cyrillic one!'

We ate, we talked and we basked in each other's company. The *zakuski* dishes were all Ukrainian specialities, a range of which surpassed the cruise ships' culinary fare—pureed herring, crispy grey mullet, a selection of sausages, *pashtet* (pate), pickles in honey and a salad of tart apples and fresh cabbage in a sour cream dressing.

The Ukraine is not called the 'breadbasket of the Soviet Union' for nothing. For centuries, the growth and harvesting of the golden grain set the rhythm of life here, and Gennadi and I were presented with a marvellous variety of different bread to accompany our meal—white, black, seeded and plaited. To prove the versatility of wheat even further, our main course was the world-famous Chicken Kiev—a glorious, breadcrumbed delight, which released warm jets of butter at the touch of our forks.

As the waiter cleared our table, I turned to Gennadi and exclaimed, 'What a delicious meal! The Ukrainians certainly know how to prepare a feast!' I also knew that this particular place would not be cheap and Gennadi would have to pay a significant sum when the bill arrived at the end of the evening. I considered privately settling this myself with the waiter but instantly registered that this gesture would not be prudent, since all Russians view hospitality in their country with such importance, my interference would be thought disrespectful.

'Now, Louisa, I would like you to taste our *varenyky*. They are so tender and delicate, they just melt in the mouth.' His face glowed with pleasure as he added, 'My mother has a recipe from my *babushka* and it is very difficult to beat.'

At that moment, the lights flickered slightly and a few gentle, musical notes filled the room, which seemed to reach out and touch my heart with soft familiarity. The source of the melody came from an instrument we both knew and loved— the *balalaika*—and the one that had brought us both together. Gennadi caught my eye and smiled, before we turned to the musician, who was dressed in an folklorically embroidered, white shirt and black loose trousers, seated on a stool near the large table of Gruziyans.

The men had stopped talking and toasting and were listening intently, as the musician suddenly burst into song. I immediately recognised a well-known romantic ballad they used to sing on the ship called *Ochi Chernye*—Dark Eyes. The lyrics had been written by a Ukrainian poet and were full of passion and longing, and this particular singer was certainly doing the song justice.

We sat very close, hands entwined, totally mesmerised by the singer's pleading words. As the tempo increased on reaching the chorus, the Gruziyans sang along, gently swaying as if in a dream, and no doubt remembering all the dark-eyed women they had left behind in their own land.

The song came to a close with rapturous applause and the singer rested and conversed with the guests, whilst the waiter brought our last course, together with tea from the large, ornate silver samovar I had noticed, as I entered the restaurant.

The *varenyky* were small dumplings of paper-thin dough, encasing a filling of soft, sweet cherries with a tiny separate jug of cherry sauce on the side—meltingly delicious, making a perfect ending to a wonderful meal. We could have stayed longer, of course, but Gennadi and I needed time to ourselves, before the evening ended and Soviet regulations came into force.

As Gennadi disappeared to pay the bill, the waiter helped me collect our belongings and I met Gennadi on the deck above. Donning our coats quickly, the cold, crisp air greeted us as we stepped out on to the gangway, and little clouds of warm breath escaped our mouths as we talked and laughed, negotiating the small, wooden walkway, as it gently rocked to and fro. I shivered slightly and Gennadi encircled me in his arm, whilst guiding me towards the road. 'Let's find a taxi quickly, before you get too cold, *lyubimaya.*'

I looked back at the ship and saw the lights flicker again, and heard the *balalaika's* sweet tone playing another famous song, *Kalinka*—a rousing folk piece known the world over, whose main refrain—*kalinka, kalinka*—increases in tempo each time it is sung. I could imagine Cossacks whirling and jumping to this music on stage, resplendent in fur hats and loose trousers, spinning faster and faster until their dance came to an abrupt and thankful end, kneeling on the floor, arms raised, chests heaving and smiling broadly with pure exhilaration.

Walking further away from the ship, the laughter and music gradually receded, until all I could hear was a faint, indistinct melody fading into the distance and dispelling into the night air. The street was quiet now and my senses seemed acutely aware of every small change the forces of nature deemed to impose. A hazy mist was rapidly sweeping in from the sea, shrouding the nearby buildings in a pale mantle and making the streetlights softly glow. The stars too, which only two hours ago, were shining so brightly in the dark, clear sky, were now being swallowed up by a mysterious gauzy veil that was reluctant to allow any light to penetrate. The sound of the traffic became strangely muted and the other few pedestrians vanished magically in the swirling fog. I felt as if we were being enveloped in a soft, damp cloud and, instinctively, tightened my hold on Gennadi's arm. He raised his other in the air, hoping to attract a late-night driver who might stop and be rewarded with a few extra clandestine roubles.

Glancing back in the direction of the ship again, I was not surprised to see that it too had taken on the appearance of a dusky apparition. Like one of those ghost ships from legends, the crew of which were enticed by beautiful, sultry sea-nymph sirens, only to end up as a shipwreck in the deadly, rocky shallows.

Suddenly out of the mist came a car, which slowed down as it approached us, headlights dimmed and engine purring softly. After a quick word with the driver, Gennadi and I sank gratefully into the back seat and we sped off in the direction of the hotel. The cold, pale fog dispersed a little as we left the locality of the harbour, and disappeared completely as we made a rapid ascent back to the city centre.

25

Alone at Last

Very soon, we arrived at my small Intourist hotel, carrying my roses and wearing my new fur hat, for which I was very grateful, now that the weather seemed to be changing for the worst. Gennadi told me that snow was indeed forecast in a day or two, but as much as I loved to see a dull landscape transform into an enchanted white world, I could also understand how unbearable it must be for most of the Soviet people, experiencing the bitter cold that came with it.

We looked at each other with a touch of shy anticipation as we entered the warmth of the hotel foyer. I wasn't quite sure what to expect, with regard to the rules for invited guests, but I was certain Gennadi would have an idea, so I waited whilst he proceeded to address the receptionist.

After a short exchange, the receptionist turned to me and said in English with a serious tone, 'No visitors allowed in the rooms after 11pm.' My eyes instantly shifted to the simple clock on the wall—just under two hours to spend with the man I adored. Then I would leave very early in the morning, to catch my plane back to Moscow, and ultimately, on to London.

Walking briskly up the stairs to the first floor, we reached the privacy of my little room and closed the door quickly and silently. My heart was beating fast now and we stood for a few seconds hugging each other tightly, not really quite believing we were completely and totally alone—at last. Then throwing our coats on the chair and kicking off our boots, we began to slowly peel off the layers of each other's clothing, with tender sensuality, until finally all that was left was the soft, welcoming warmth of skin touching skin.

As if in a dream, my body was lifted and placed gently on the little single bed. Gennadi's dark eyes, full of longing and desire, never left mine for a moment as his soft lips hovered above my face then dipped down to meet my own, in a long, lingering, passionately possessive, kiss—the kiss I had been dreaming of since we had been parted all those weeks ago.

My body shivered with pleasure as his lips moved to my neck, still kissing, and onto my breasts until he was kissing every part of my exposed and willing nakedness. I was fully aroused, as was he, but I felt we needed to take our time and enjoy our bodies totally before our lovemaking reached its peak. Gennadi recognised this, and we continued to explore and caress with great care, knowing each other's bodies well enough to give and receive unmeasured, selfless satisfaction. Then when delay was no longer an option, we drew each other close, firmly and with purposeful consent, joining at last, one beautiful entity, moving in perfect rhythm, reaching heights I never dared imagine or even dreamt about. I was riding on the crest of a gigantic wave and Gennadi was with me reaching ever higher, when all too soon on reaching the summit and restraint was impossible, a series of delicious rapid waves swept over and through me, engulfing my very soul. We gasped in unison and were left breathless, both spent, clinging fiercely to each other and wishing this moment would endure forever.

But time was not our friend that night and as we reluctantly disentangled our entwined bodies, I glanced at my watch on the bedside table and said quickly. 'Let's shower together, Gennadi. Something we never had time for on the ship. A new sensation before you go.'

He smiled and took my hand as we entered the simple little shower room and ran the water till it was warm and our skin, slick with soap, slid luxuriously over the other, until it was impossible not to make love all over again. How we wished time would just stand still and these moments could be enjoyed all over again. But lingering too long could easily cause trouble, if noticed. So, with a heavy sigh, Gennadi reluctantly reached for a towel. 'I have to leave now, *lyubimaya*, Louisa,' he said sadly, as he hurried to dry himself and hastily pull on his clothes and warm leather boots. 'But I will come early and join you for breakfast. Please don't come down now. I will be here at 6.30 in reception. I love you, Louisa, even more after today.'

'I feel the same, Gennadi. I just want the time to know you totally and absolutely.'

We kissed again and he turned quickly to go, leaving me with beautiful memories, all of which I knew I would relive for the best part of my last night in Odessa.

26

Farewell

Hurrying down the stairs to the lobby very early the next day, with my two bags, my new fur hat, and coat draped over one arm, I greeted the receptionist who took my order for breakfast and disappeared into the kitchen. As reluctant as I was to part with my beautiful roses, I realised that they would probably not survive a long journey, so I left them in the room for the chambermaid when she came to tidy. I knew Gennadi would not mind.

No sooner had I settled down at one of the three little tables laid for breakfast, when Gennadi walked briskly through the door, looking flushed with cold and wearing the same knee-length, black leather coat as yesterday but now with added scarf and gloves. His face instantly broke into a smile on seeing me and I was quickly engulfed in a firm but tender embrace.

'It's very cold today, Louisa,' he said, removing his coat, scarf and gloves to sit beside me just before breakfast arrived—a welcome cup of tea for us both and fresh bread rolls, honey and a selection of sliced cheese and salami. He took my hand and squeezed it gently and I smiled back asking, 'Weren't there any taxis today, Gennadi?'

'Not one. I caught a tram, then walked the rest of the way. It's very busy at this time, with people travelling to work and many of the buses and trams are overloaded.' I knew this to be true but it appeared to me that any time of day seemed to cause the local transport to be particularly crowded.

We were both very much aware of our imminent separation and, as we talked and drank our tea and ate our crispy bread rolls, our faces could not hide the sadness we were inevitably feeling. Then out of the blue, some gentle music drifted through from the reception area and we both looked up towards the sound, surprised but delighted, to hear once more the familiar strums of a *balalaika*. It seemed that once again, memories of our first illicit meeting on the *Ukraina* came flooding back, when we were instantly and physically attracted to each other, amidst the music and noise of a typical Russian crew party in full swing. And added to this was the heightened sense of risk involved, should we choose to abandon all we had been taught to adhere to.

'Gennadi, do you still play your *balalaika*?' I asked, curiously. 'You have real talent, you know. Maybe you should be a musician instead of an electrician—or both,' I added, trying to sound light-hearted.

'No, Louisa,' he replied, solemnly, 'it was involved in an accident and is completely beyond repair.'

Shocked, I asked him what had happened and as he began the story, I glimpsed a flicker of emotion and regret pass fleetingly over his handsome features. I knew this instrument had been an important part of his social life for many years, but I also realised that it had played a major role in bringing us both together.

So, he told me the story of the night on board when a good friend of his, Pavel, was due to play in the *balalaika* ensemble for the passengers in the crew show. Pavel had been rehearsing in his cabin when he accidentally broke a string and didn't have a replacement, so rushing to Gennadi's cabin, he had asked to borrow his instrument for the show and Gennadi had, of course, agreed.

The show had gone well but Pavel had to dash to serve at the late-night buffet in the restaurant and left Gennadi's *balalaika* on the bandstand, intending to collect it later. Unfortunately, someone had got there first, according to another crew member, who was in the room clearing the tables for the evening. An inebriated passenger had spotted it and proceeded, with great interest, to pick it up and decide to try his hand at a bit of playing. This, inevitably, turned out to be a complete fiasco, and cursing loudly, flung the instrument down onto the wooden dance floor, where it cracked and almost split in two, before the man marched off in the direction of the nearest bar.

This was where it was found by the unlucky Pavel half an hour later, who was mortified, to say the very least. It would take a very long time for Pavel to save up and repay Gennadi for his loss. Gennadi told him not to worry, as he probably wouldn't play the *balalaika* again anyway after he left the ship.

I was horrified and, experiencing a mixture of fury and grief, took Gennadi's hands in mine and said, 'I am so very sorry, my love. Can it really not be repaired?'

He looked at me with a steady gaze and, smiling slightly at my concern, said, 'No, Louisa. I will have to find another, one day—maybe.' Then added, with a wider smile and determined look, 'But it is not important right now, I have found you and that is all I need.'

I hugged and held him close, just as the phone in reception rang with a noisy clatter, that made us both jump and spring guiltily apart. Then, much to my surprise, the receptionist called out 'A phone call for you, Miss Bennett.'

It could only be one person. 'Hello darling, it's me,' said Dermot cheerfully. 'Katya and I will accompany you to the airport in half an hour. See you shortly!' and rang off.

All too soon, our time together was over and I was left alone on the pavement whilst Gennadi headed into the city centre, to report for duty at the large hotel where he was currently employed as resident electrician. We had said our tearful farewells and promised to keep in touch by post and telegram, with news of his impending divorce and my own arrangements for the next visit. We both had a lot of paperwork to complete over the following weeks, and my last vision of him was of a man striding purposefully away, shoulders square and firm, with a look of resolution, turning back only once, before hailing a taxi and disappearing round a corner. I felt suddenly very cold and stepped back inside the hotel to wait for my friends, and was sincerely grateful that I would not be alone on the first part of my long journey home, for they would try and keep me focused on positive thoughts.

My eyes were still watering and I was beginning to have a sinking feeling in the pit of my stomach. I couldn't stop myself from imagining that this could be the last time we ever saw each other. I certainly wasn't sure if my visa would be granted. I also began to have serious doubts about our proposed plans, which might very well be thwarted, when suddenly, a small Lada hastily drew up beside the kerb and screeched to a halt. Out jumped Dermot with a jolly smile.

'Morning darling. Let's get your bags loaded. You sit in the back with Katya whilst I keep the driver company. With legs as long as mine, I don't think I should risk the back seat— tried it once and my knees ended up under my chin! Couldn't straighten them out properly for days,' he added with a silly grin.

I laughed and squeezed in beside Katya before heading off in the direction of the airport, our little car jostling amidst the busy traffic of cars, trams and buses that were still ferrying people to work at this early hour. We chatted all the way about their plans for the future, and they both offered to help Gennadi, even if it just meant moral support, whenever it was needed. They were sure it wouldn't be long before we would all meet again—we just had to show patience, perseverance and tolerance. Wise words which gave me some comfort as I made my way to departures, waving at my two dear friends, with whom I had shared so much, arms around each other's waists and waving back, looking incredibly relaxed and undeniably, blissfully happy.

27

The Adventure Continues

On reaching my homeland once more, the first two days were occupied with constant chat and discussion, as I related all that had taken place since I last saw my parents. They were almost as excited as me when they learnt of the meeting with Gennadi at Katya's house and were happy to share my joy.

When they were then briefed on my immediate plans, they asked me about the future and where we would both live, if given a choice. Their home, which was in fact a small hotel on the moors of Exmoor, would be available without question until Gennadi and I could afford to be independent. But that option may not arise if Gennadi was forbidden to leave the Soviet Union and we were both forced to remain in Russia. This concept continued to worry me and many times I had questioned Dermot regarding this dilemma, but he was unable to help me.

'Watch this space, darling! Time is the only answer to your question. If it works for Katya and me, then undoubtedly, you will follow with Gennadi.'

I was also constantly reminded of Gennadi's gentle warning, that I had to be unwaveringly positive about my marriage to him. He would be totally reliant on me to begin with, if we were allowed to leave Russia and live in England. He could not speak the English language yet and would know no one in order to work and make a life there. A huge responsibility on my part, but one I was more than willing to take on. I was very sure of this.

Gennadi and I had also talked about living in the Soviet Union, if necessary, and he was concerned that it could prove difficult for me, being used to a Western lifestyle. Would our relationship suffer if I was not happy? I had assured him that I would work as hard as possible to make our marriage a success and I would have Dermot for company and inspiration. I thought of Stefan and how he had lived happily for many years in this communist country and was able to travel often to the West, to see friends and family. I hoped this would apply to me as well.

On the fifth day at home, a telegram arrived from Odessa, saying all was well. How incredibly happy I was! A sure sign that our correspondence was permitted, and I immediately sent one back.

I had begun to fill in visa forms and look at flights, as well as contacting the Foreign Office in London. Dermot had advised me to obey all the legalities and request the documents I needed to apply for the permission to marry a Soviet citizen. The local parish church near my home was issuing the banns for our proposed betrothal and I felt that the formalities on my side were well underway.

Then about a week after my return, I received an unexpected phone call from my boss. Hearing his voice again revived the uncomfortable sense of guilt which still haunted me when I considered the serious repercussions the Soviets could have taken against his company. His whole business could have been ruined. I had spoken to him briefly on returning home from the *Ukraina* and apologised sincerely for what had happened on board, but he had assured me that no harm had been done and future contracts with the Black Sea Company remained in force, providing I did not return to this shipping line.

He asked me how I was feeling and if I was ready to start work again soon.

'Oh,' I gasped, 'I didn't expect to be back on the ships quite so soon. What did you have in mind?' I added politely, envisaging the time it would take me to finish all the documents for the Odessa visit.

I was ready to decline this generous offer when he continued, 'Well, Louisa, you would be working alone this time as the ship is quite small, about a hundred and fifty passengers, and it belongs to the Baltic fleet. Consequently, you would be cruising the Northern Capitals of Scandinavia and ending up in Leningrad, the ship's home port.'

At the mention of this last city, my mind and heart began to speed up considerably.

'Leningrad?' I asked quickly. 'Are the ships Russian-registered?'

'Yes, this is a smaller Russian cruise line but nonetheless popular, especially with the British public. As you will be visiting a Soviet city again, we will make sure you have your own visa to avoid any difficulties, so you can accompany the passengers ashore and make the most of the tours. The ship sets sail from Tilbury in two weeks. What do you say?'

I was lost for words, and as he waited for a reply, my mind began to form new plans and possibilities for meeting Gennadi in another city, much sooner than I could have hoped. Although he was forbidden to leave the Soviet Union, he was still allowed to travel within it, and I could see no reason why he could not meet me in Leningrad. I would have my own visa in two weeks' time and would not have to worry about the chance of one not being granted. It sounded too good a chance to miss.

'It sounds perfect,' I replied confidently, 'thank you for thinking of me. Can I please confirm it in two or three days?'

'Yes, Louisa, of course. I know how much you have enjoyed working on the Russian ships and I have heard that you are learning the language—always appreciated by the Soviet crew. Call me in a couple of days.'

Putting the phone down with mounting excitement, my heart thumping in my chest, I jumped in the car and headed for the post office to send an important telegram. I didn't expect an immediate reply as I knew Gennadi was working and could not always get to the post office. But two days later, I received a huge surprise. I was in my room when the phone rang and shortly after, my dad called up the stairs saying it was for me, from Odessa. I leapt off the bed and tore down the stairs, sliding off the last two in my hurry to get to the phone. How could Gennadi actually call me or was it someone else? Dermot, Katya or an official from the registry office? I tentatively put the receiver to my ear. '*Da*,' I said nervously.

'Louisa, *dorogaya*,' said Gennadi's familiar voice. A thrill of excitement surged through me.

'Gennadi, it's wonderful to hear your voice. I never thought it possible!'

He laughed and said, 'I received your message and will arrange a flight to Leningrad in three weeks. I have some friends there who will let me stay the night. I will come to meet your new ship and I'll probably have some important news for you as well.'

We spoke a little then about our families, before his time was up and his call ended.

I was deliriously happy and felt that good fortune was once again on my side. The foundations for our future together were definitely falling into place and I felt sure that my longed-for destiny could indeed be achieved.

I had one more important task to arrange before I left home. Reaching for the phone book, I dialled a well-known music shop in London and asked if they stocked Russian *balalaikas*. Of course, they said, only the best quality instruments from Russian craftsmen. 'Excellent,' I replied, 'I'll be up to visit your shop next week.'

The End

Bibliography

Thayer, C. W. (1961) *Russia, The Sunday Times World Library,* United States.

Papashvily, H. and G. (1972) *The Cooking of Russia,* United States.

Massie, S. (1980) *Land of the Firebird, The Beauty of Old Russia*, London.